A BLIND DATE WITH DESTINY

Also by Steve Macfarlane

The Carver Device Series Books

A Blind Date with Destiny

The Carver Device

For more information visit smilingtigermedia.com

ISBN 978-1-7637099-0-4 (eBook)
ISBN 978-1-7637099-1-1 (Paperback)

A Blind Date with Destiny

STEVE MACFARLANE

A story never starts from the beginning.

It is just one story

in the midst of

all the lives and places

in every other story.

This one of course, could never happen.

CONTENTS

Forward

He woke to the sound of the smoke alarm
and the smell of burnt toast.

Ahhh, he thought, it's nice to be home.

| 1 |

They meet

20 odd years ago

Ray Barton wasn't known for strong opinions. In fact, he was well known for sitting on the fence. Over time that fence had been rustic, plastic, caustic and finally toxic, so in recent years he decided to put some effort into making the fence more comfortable, he wasn't getting off it now. He'd wondered about finding some moral high ground but it seemed like a lot of effort and so he hadn't bothered so far.

His parents had loved him more than evolution required and that had created a unique set of problems. While they encouraged positive thinking, they also thought that an understanding of risk management was important. In preparation for the life his parents had foreseen, he'd been sent to a disaster management course. The school had burnt down during the second term which sort of set the tone for the next few years.

He'd written a book "The Art and Optimism of Cord Wiggling" which had been a surprising success. His publisher had been keen for him to write another one but he couldn't come up with another title that good again.

Elizabeth Buchanan was from a small town in Scotland so unfortunately, she was usually called Macbeth when out of earshot, although she always called herself Liz. The reports of her beauty varied wildly and were largely dependent on distance from her and the viewer's optician's prescription. Some called her a rugged beauty but not usually to her face.

One of her hobbies was doing things that scared the bejesus out of agnostics. As a supporter of her local atheist's group, she liked giving agnostics an opportunity to confront the question and really get to grips with their true feelings. It was rumoured she was getting a healthy commission.

Ray and Liz went to a small restaurant for their first date. Not too fancy but cosy and sympathetically lit. It was between the Christian Fish and Chip shop, 'The Lord Giveth and Takeaway' and the darts themed pub on the corner, known as 'Tossers'.

Ray talked about his love of language and got in the one about the first person who saw and named a shark by trying to say shit and fark at the same time. She'd snorted then laughed. An infectious, gurgly, uninhibited sound that he enjoyed a lot. He liked making her laugh.

At seemingly random intervals, a waiter exploded out of the swinging doors, carrying an assortment of trays. He was on a mission and from the look on his face, it was a serious mission.

He was an interesting character study. As he approached the first table, his expression changed from the 'serious on a mission' face, to the 'come into my warm embrace' benevolent face that was delighted to see each and every one of them and that time was of no concern. As soon as this was completed, he moved on to the next table. You could watch the serious face return for a brief moment as he got his bearings and then on to the next table and back to full beam. It was exhausting to watch. Mildly entertaining but exhausting. A bit like some jazz.

The waiter arrived at their table, beamed at them and presented menus while declaring "Welcome, tonight the chef's specials are on the board over there. I will give you a few moments to make your minds up… and remember, if you need anything… I'm Jack. He beamed again and evaporated into the darkness behind a pillar.

"Wow", said Ray," I've never met a conditional identity before. I wonder who he is if we don't need anything."

Liz looked up from her menu, nodding and smiling sympathetically, acknowledging the joke, "That's not bad."

As they studied the menus, Liz mused conspiratorially, "I hear that all the food on the menu has been killed naturally."

Ray said slowly, "I'm not entirely sure what that means?"

"Me neither", said Liz, "but it's got nature in it. Surely that must be good?"

"Does it mean the food died of natural causes?", asked Ray, "Isn't that roadkill?"

She looked at him, smiled, and said, "Entree?"

"On tray?", he repeated, returning the smile, "I'm usually happy to have it 'on plate', but I'm willing to try new things."

She smiled back, pleased to be flirting again.

They watched and listened to the family at the table next to them noisily and aggressively devouring a substantial pile of recently deceased seafood before giving their order to the now returned and hovering waiter. They thought of him as Jack because they needed something and it seemed appropriate. There was some brief speculation about whether his name actually changed as soon as they didn't need anything. This was heading in Schrodinger and his theoretical cat territory and they both knew that was a road to argument.

Their thick steaks were mouth-wateringly tender and stole much of the conversation as it moved from an initial focus on how wonderful they were, to, how long do you have to hang a steak to get it to be that tender and by extension, how long since it had been in a field and finally, what state was it in before they scraped off all the muck?

The mental pictures and answers to those questions unsettled the equilibrium and cast a temporary gloom that was magically brought back on track when in desperation Liz asked if Ray had any hobbies. This opened a floodgate and soon they were exploring areas of common interest.

As dessert arrived Ray had that memorable 'Matrix' moment. He turned to Jack the waiter while struggling to contain a huge grin and said... "there is no spoon". This had been witty, poignant and charming, creating a special moment between them. In fact, they absolutely pissed themselves... to the point where they were asked to be quiet or leave. Laughing's always funnier when you can't or shouldn't.

After regaining some composure, they discovered a mutual love of science-fiction, comedy and detective mystery stories which was sealed when they realised they had both created and used the same special sign-off.

'May the force be with you as you live long and prosper'.

The thought of marriage had crossed Ray's mind like an elderly pedestrian trying to herd a group of cats across a busy highway. Slowly, uncertainly and with a mixture of delight, horror and a growing inevitability.

They married three years later in a science fiction themed wedding, much to their delight and Liz's mother's disgust.

| 2 |

Friday phone call

The Present

As usual at this time on a Friday night, Liz rang her mother for their weekly catch up and chat.

"Have you heard?" asked her mother, firing the first shot, "I think your friend Mary from school is marrying a Moslem. I overheard her mother in the supermarket. A woman asked who Mary was marrying and I'm pretty sure she said he was called Asif."

Finding herself temporarily speechless, Liz just let the silence ring out until her mother continued with... "Anyway, your Aunty June is getting worse and looks like a transplant is her best option now."

Aunty June was one of her mother's two sisters. Aunty April and Aunty June had married cousins and they became Liz's two uncles, Horry and Morty, which was easier to say than Horace and Mortimer. Forever known in family circles as Horrified and Mortified.

Liz said, "I thought her daughter was prepared to donate her kidneys."

"No, she actually said she was prepared to donate her kids," her mother responded dourly.

"Ha Ha". Liz made the absolute minimum sound required to be considered a laugh.

"While this was sort of amusing it wasn't very helpful. So, the search goes on. At least there's still a lighter side, although now she's really worried about dying."

"Why?" asked Liz.

"The doctor told her that she would have to take one of these tablets every day for the rest of her life", her mother declared deflatedly.

"Okay, so what's that got to do with it?", Liz wasn't following the gist of the conversation.

"The prescription was for 1 packet of 36 tablets. She thinks she's got less than 36 days to live. I try to tell her about the repeat bit, but she just won't listen."

"Aren't you worried about the nocebo effect?", asked Liz.

"What's that?", her mother asked, "I've never heard of it. Is it like placebo?"

"It's more commonly called medical hexing or belief-based harm," said Liz, "It's basically when a patient believes absolutely in the authority of a doctor and if the doctor says they only have 1 month to live, then somehow or other they fall off the perch after a month."

Liz could hear the disapproval in her mother's voice.

"That's not a nice expression Liz. Fall off the perch. Where did you get that from?"

"Not sure Ma, must have picked it up at work," Liz added sheepishly, still amazed that her mother could make her feel like a small child again, just with the tone of her voice.

"Anyway, that's about it for me", declared her mother, "What about your news dear?"

"Ray's heading off on another trip soon," Liz mused, "He's travelling most weeks for the next month or so as some people are interested in some of his ideas. My childhood pen pal, the Great Dane, will be in town for a couple of days and we've been getting the spare room ready."

"I liked her, she was a lot of fun. How long is she staying?", asked her mother.

"Just for the weekend", said Liz, "she's stopping over on her way to some conference".

"What about work?" her mother asked.

"The usual", said Liz, "You know, it's been quite a week at the paper. The girl who does the births is pregnant, the position's vacant ad job is still not filled and the guy who looks after the obituaries doesn't look well… Boom Boom."

"Huh", was the best her mother could muster.

"On a more serious note, the strangest news is that somehow I've been selected as a *'mystery shopper'* for the Adult Services section. What's that all about? Is it punishment? Reward? I really don't understand. Why me?"

"Now dear", her mother said reassuringly, "you just have to resolve to put it out of your head the best you can until next week when you're back at work. No good will come from fretting about it."

"Thanks Ma", said Liz, "I know... I will…" (knowing she wouldn't).

"Have a great week. Love you heaps". Her mother hung up without waiting for a reply.

"Bye", said Liz, fairly sure that she was talking to herself.

She returned to the living room where Ray was standing over the coffee table playing the last post on a pretend trumpet.

"What on earth are you doing?", she asked.

He grinned a mischievous grin, "All the batteries in the remote died. I just thought they needed a proper send-off."

She responded with a weak smile.

"How's your Mum?", he asked.

"Intolerant", Liz declared.

"What? Gluten?" asked Ray, concerned.

"No... just generally intolerant." Liz delivered this with a world weariness in her voice that Ray noticed had been increasing over recent years.

Ray pictured his mother-in-law. She'd say things like, "Half the time I have no idea what I'm doing", seemingly unaware that if this could be proven, then under the current laws and thinking, she should be institutionalised.

It amazed him how often people say these sorts of things and we just think they're trying to be humorous. Was it really a cry for help? On reflection, he probably wondered about it too often, and with too much hopefulness.

| 3 |

Cleaning out the spare room

Saturday Morning

Ray spent most of Saturday morning clearing out the spare room for their visitor. As it happened, he'd completely misunderstood when Liz had talked lovingly about her Great Dane. Turned out to be a very large woman from Denmark.

This had forced a quick mental review of all the stories about the Great Dane as somehow, they'd still made sense when he thought they were about a dog. He was absolutely positive he could remember being told that she had done well at Crufts one year. Maybe that was the wrong clue?

Anyway, when he mentioned it to his doctor, he'd told him he was suffering from a case of anagnorisis and that he should look it up when he got home.

Looking around the room he was initially overwhelmed by the piles of old clothes and linen, boxes and suitcases, books, magazines and old board games. Looking more closely revealed suitcases, abandoned hobbies and projects, musical instrument cases, unused exercise equipment and unspecified bags. The spare bed was under that lot somewhere. In their house, this room had become the black hole of forgotten things.

Perhaps they needed another spare room?

Ray began picking up loose items and trying to find somewhere to store or hide them. The strategy was basically Russian dolls. Will one item fit inside another? Not throwing anything away but take up less space. After a while he stood back and surveyed the room. It still looked like a complete mess.

As he moved old boxes and bits of computers, he was wrestling with a lifelong bad habit. Trying to make a decision without closing off any options. It was a game he'd played since childhood. This was procrastination as a learned skill and practised craft.

As with many things in life, he was a slow learner. Some of his mistakes he'd enjoyed so much he'd done them over and over again. That's one of the tricky bits, it's so hard to give up things you really enjoy... even love.

For the umpteenth time, he moved the extra large bonsai tree. He looked at it closely. It's getting bigger and heavier every time I do this, he thought. In its present state can it still be called a bonsai tree? It was looking less like a miniature tree and more like something his old teacher used to call a bonsai train-wreck.

He picked up an old-fashioned floral suitcase when it unexpectedly fell open and deposited its content all over the floor.

"Shit!"

It was mostly papers and photos and loose items, so they went everywhere. A quick inspection showed it to be stuff from Liz's childhood. Old school reports, artwork and some of her early stories. I wonder how long since she's seen any of this?

Then he discovered a little gem. It was a set list for one of Liz's early bands. This was long before he knew her. She'd talked about playing in a band in high school but he'd never seen a set list.

- Smells Like Teen Spirit - Nirvana
- Celebrity Skin - Hole
- Seether - Veruca Salt
- Rebel Girl - Bikini Kill
- Grunge Disney Medley
- Zombie - The Cranberries
- Just a Girl - No Doubt
- Cannonball - The Breeders
- Grunge The Little Mermaid Medley
- Only Happy When It Rains - Garbage

He smiled. What rebels they must have been. Attached to the setlist was a photo of the band. They all looked so young. He could recognise Molly, Liz and Sarah. He'd never met the other girl. He couldn't remember her name. She hadn't made old bones. The girls had been heavy drinkers at one point. They all stopped except the girl whose name he couldn't remember. Unfortunately, she passed away in her mid-forties. He kept the setlist and photo aside to show Liz. Hopefully it will be a happy memory.

He then opened the door to the walk-in wardrobe and did a week's worth of cardio by walking into a large spider's web. His body agreed that he should be somewhere else and each body part had its own idea about where that should be as he tried to go in several directions at the same time.

He sat down heavily on the corner of the spare bed for a short rest while his heart rate returned to normal. Whew! I had no idea I was going to get such a workout from this.

The radio began trumpeting the 'Majestic Fanfare' to indicate it was time for the hourly news broadcast. He half listened and it seemed to confirm his belief that the government was continuing their tributes to classic BBC radio shows with another round from 'I'm sorry I haven't a clue'. Their energy policy seemed to be based on generating power from our ancestors spinning in the graves. He switched the radio off and returned to his own thoughts.

Had he and Liz really been together for 20 years? Some serious cracks were starting to appear in the facade of their relationship.

Every now and then, Liz would get really down. She didn't want to talk about it and he didn't want to push, assuming they had the sort of relationship where she would talk about it when she was ready. After 20 years, she still wasn't ready. Not to talk to him anyway.

She'd lost her best friend years ago during surgery in a *'never event'.* An event that should never happen. Something had gone wrong and she'd never recovered. The loss of her friend had rocked Liz's world completely. How do you ever get over the death of a close friend? Your best friend. That was his best guess but it was more than that.

Liz attacked religion and the religious often. He'd tried many times to get her to explain the source of this level of passion, but she always became incoherent and white with rage. He could recognise trauma but didn't really know what to do about it.

He persevered for quite a few years thinking that she would unburden herself but each time the trauma was re-lived and eventually he gave up as it seemed to make her worse, not better. If the cure is worse than the disease, then another approach is needed. He decided to let sleeping dogs lie.

She seemed to enjoy arguing with people of faith and had her arsenal of lines and stories. She admired atheists like Christopher Hitchens and Richard Dawkins. Not necessarily because they were right but because of the way they constructed their arguments and were fearless in attacking dogma. If she could get some humour in, all the better.

It seemed to her that the reason for most of the world's problems was that even though the bible says the meek will inherit the earth, people ever since then have made it their mission to make sure they don't inherit the earth in '*their*' generation or their kids. This can has been kicked down the road for at least 2000 years.

Liz used to say she had an extreme fear of heights and so it was unlikely she'd ever be able to go to heaven... it was just too high up. An acrophobic in heaven would be an eternal panic attack which seems like a bad deal. Another favourite was about the Jews being lost in the desert for 40 years and why men just won't stop and ask for directions.

He'd read somewhere that 82% of women were better patients than your average man. Liz was in the other 18%. Ray had tried many times to care for her when she was ill or injured but she was a terrible patient, moving effortlessly between her four native homeostatic states. Grumpy, sleepy, psychotic and medicated.

One time when she had a serious cold, he'd spent the afternoon looking for loopholes in the marriage contract. He still couldn't find where he'd agreed to some of the things that apparently, he had, which made him wonder why the marriage vows aren't prefaced in the same way as an arrest.

"Anything you say or do will be taken down and may be used in evidence against you at a later date". Perhaps it was time for a new marriage vow that was a bit more realistic and included clauses like, it is perfectly okay to be psychotic every now and then. It's part of human nature and shouldn't be seen as an affliction or disability in any way.

When he'd looked it up, divorce rates were pretty horrific. First marriages only survive about half the time and the stats get worse for second and third attempts. It's hard not to see that as a learning curve. Monogamy is difficult. It's harder to do the right thing, to keep the vows we make. That's why so few people do it. It's so much harder to have integrity.

There seems to be assumptions that most men aren't capable of being faithful. He didn't believe that to be true as most women aren't capable of being faithful either but always for more sophisticated reasons.

Early in their marriage, Liz had referred to him as her "drop of golden sun" which had always made him smile. It was several years before he was stuck in a hotel room and bored enough to think he could watch the Sound of Music all the way through. He got as far as the Do-Re-Mi song and had to rethink the marriage.

He'd been in a few romantic relationships before Liz, the longest was in his late teens and to a girl he first met on a train. She appeared to be powered by sneezes. He'd watched transfixed by the changes of expressions that were charging through her face. He struggled to comprehend how so many different emotions could be expressed in such a short space of time and how expressively. Beautiful and ugly, harsh and soft.

As he watched, he noticed that there seemed to be some sort of cycle to it. After a sneeze explosion, there was a brief look of relief as all the tensions drained from her face and made her beautiful. This was followed by the *'Oh no, it's going to happen again'* look.

A slowly creeping look of dread as the realisation the next sneeze is getting ready to happen, the tensing of the body, the hardening of the face, the desperate look around for anything that can help... and finally that look of resignation that it's going to happen, going to hurt and there is absolutely nothing she can do about it.

He watched her go through the cycle 3 times before feeling that he had to say something. It only occurred to him later that he should have said something funny or clever or endearing but that also revealed a bit about him.

He blurted... "That is amazing!"

She looked up, directly into his eyes and pleadingly winced in his general direction and that was it... He was in love!

His attention returned to the spare room. He realised that he was sitting with his legs spread wide, silently airing his opinions to the empty room.

"What'd happened?" He asked silently and rhetorically.

"Life... I s'pose", an internal voice responded.

He got up and went to the laundry to check on the washing. The load was finished so he transferred the clothes to the dryer. That done, he opened the washing machine and threw the next load of clothes in, optimistically squirting in some stuff that looked like it was meant to be a part of the washing cycle. Couldn't hurt, surely?

He walked back to the kitchen, grabbed a beer, some nuts, sat down in his favourite chair and switched on the TV. He was enjoying cracking walnuts and peanuts with his beer. There's something really nice about opening the shell using a nutcracker. It took him back to his childhood when it was a real treat. He looked at the nutcracker curiously. What a simple invention that has stood the test of time. As idiot proof as you can get.

Then he pinched his finger in a partly cracked walnut. It was surprisingly painful. He reviewed and revised his memories as quickly as he manually pulled the walnut apart. A few seconds ago I would have said that was impossible. Sucking the end of the affected finger he considered the advantages of pre-shelled walnuts. He was lost in this quandary when Liz came in.

"The Great Dane will be here at 4 o'clock next Saturday", said Liz, "Are you okay to drive me to the airport and pick her up?" "You don't have to come into the airport but it would be a great help not to have to park".

"Yeh sure", said Ray.

"Thanks darling", Liz said and kissed him on the top of his head.

As Liz left, he returned to his ruminating. He wasn't over the hill. Mind you, he acknowledged that the hill was in sight and looming large as they say. Recently, Liz seemed to be communicating with him using some form of morse code with dots and dashes being replaced with grunts and scowls. Something is going on there, so it's probably a good idea to lay low for a bit.

He looked up through the window and noticed his neighbour was packing boxes into her car. He smiled, she was the *'good'* neighbour, Carol. The guy on the other side was one of those English people who love to hate the French. He keeps mentioning Agincourt in casual conversation. The man absolutely refused to be an entrepreneur, eat French fries in a café, have déjà vu or rendezvous with anyone. He just wouldn't have anything to do with any word that contained an accent, grave or circumflex. Ray and Liz used to joke that he probably drank *'bitter'* and only played sports where he could have the *'right wing'* position. For some unfathomable reason he felt the need to mention how much he hated the French at every opportunity. Ray and Liz called it *'The English disease'*.

They reasoned that there was probably a really good explanation or story behind it all but neither were interested enough to put themselves through the ordeal of asking the question and having to be present for the response. If they could get the shorthand version, it might be mildly interesting but until then, they just smiled, waved and tried really hard not to get caught in a situation where a conversation was impossible to avoid. It didn't always work.

What is it with people who start a sentence with, 'I'm not a *'insert a word like troll, bitch, racist, bigot, or similar ... BUT...'* and then go on to talk about all the things they said they weren't or wouldn't.

As he watched Carol pull out onto the street, he casually wondered why his '*good*' neighbour was home at this time? It's odd. I wonder what's up?

Carol's husband was an interesting character. That weird combination of bookworm and superhero. His name was Eric but Liz had nicknamed him "Conan the Librarian". He did something at the Uni. They had a nice kid too. A boy, maybe 7 or 8. They all seemed happy.

He'd been married to Liz for nearly 20 years, through thick and a lot of thin. Now the challenge was to remember why they bothered. In the beginning, they'd had one of those relationships where their love became a secret society of two. Intoxicating and dangerous. He was worried lately that they'd just become two people who lived in the same house and knew most of the people in the other's stories. Was that enough anymore?

The other night when he was wandering around the internet, he came across DNA testing kits as a novel gift idea. The first one he found was *23andMe* but there were lots to choose from. It was late and that thing where, the later it is, the better the idea is, seemed to be working. On reflection, that wasn't quite right. Was it, ideas seem better if they come at you faster?

Anyway, he bought kits for himself and Liz as that neatly covered Christmas presents for that year. He was quite excited about the idea as he really didn't know much about his family history.

Apparently, both his grandfathers were bottle collectors. One actually collected old bottles of all types and the other collected them after he'd drunk the contents. His dad's father obviously had some issues. His father rarely mentioned him and his grandmother was hard to get onto topics like that. She'd died when he was in his twenties and she'd only wanted to talk about when he was going to get a haircut, stop messing about with music, find a nice girl and similar pressing matters. His other grandparents were nice people but they didn't know or care for long dead relatives. They took more interest in living ones.

Anyway, when he mentioned the DNA kits to Liz, he hadn't received the reaction he'd hoped for. In fact, it appeared to cast a bit of gloom over the day. He noticed that Liz seemed unusually distracted.

She'll talk when she's ready, he thought optimistically.

| 4 |

Give a dog a bad name

Saturday Afternoon

Liz was standing at the back door about to shout at the top of her voice when it began dawning on her some of the disadvantages to calling the new pup '*Shagger*'.

It was some sort of unhealthy competition thing between siblings. Liz had an older sister and a younger brother, but she rarely saw him. There'd always been competition between the sisters and though they were very different types of people, it remained an issue. If one did something silly and a bit daring, the other felt compelled to top it. Coming up with ridiculous names for pets had seemed fairly harmless when they were kids but it'd really gotten out of hand now.

There'd been so many times. Once when she was younger, her sister had asked her to take a friend's dog to the beach. Another one of her sister's '*jokes*'. She'd agreed to take him as she loved dogs and just as she was leaving, her sister said, "They named him after the basketball player Shaquille O'Neale, but they mostly call him '*Shaq*'". In complete innocence, Liz had let him off the leash and started playing throw the ball games with him. After a while the dog got distracted and so she called him back. This caused a panic amongst the people around her that completely took her by surprise. She imploded internally trying to process that her saying "Shaq" to get the dog back was being interpreted by the people around her as "Shark", and they were looking for it and freaking out about people currently in the water.

Hysteria seems to travel even faster than Covid misinformation.

In an impossibly short time, the cry of "Shark" had multiplied as helpful people joined in, increasing the volume, hysteria and general confusion. Some other helpful person threw in, "I think I saw it. I think it's over there" pointing at the sea.

Amongst the confusion, Shaq had found another dog to play with and was blissfully unaware of any problem. Liz was able to catch him, attach his leash and quietly walk away as the crowd on the beach became more anxious because they could no longer see the shark. Where would it pop up next? The crowd had whipped itself into a complete frenzy and created a palpable tension entirely based on a single word.

As Liz walked home, it hit her like a flash. Her sister knew something like this would happen. She'd done it on purpose as some sort of joke. She would have known that even though it was against the rules, Liz would let the dog off the leash. How should she respond to this? If she were to tell her what actually happened then she would know that she "*got*" her. It wasn't like it was the first time.

Her older sister had developed fairly large breasts in her teens and when she felt in the mood, she'd wear a specially constructed bra that had the nipples built in... just at impossibly weird angles. It had the effect that when people looked at her breasts while pretending not to, they would involuntarily double take as they processed what they were seeing.

She did things like this all the time. If there was a way to shock you, she absolutely loved it. *'Outrageous behaviour being rewarded will not help her'*, her grandmother used to say, but that advice was overlooked as terms like *precocious* and *flamboyant* were bandied around.

Growing up, you would have thought that she would be gay or bi-sexual or something but she wasn't. That wasn't her thing. She'd become an artist. That wasn't too surprising and like many of that persuasion, she'd enjoyed *'aids to creativity'*. In her youth, the *'aids to creativity'* had overtaken her life for a while and it seemed that only an accident of fate had let her slip through that phase, relatively unscathed. Nowadays, she had a more modest attitude towards *'aids to creativity'* and used them infrequently.

Infrequently.

That word had taken on such a specific meaning in her family because of one particular joke. It made it an awkward and unusual word to use now as it always invoked the joke as it's such a beautiful example of how humour works through language alone.

The joke was "An older couple meet on a date and start talking through various topics and attitudes and they eventually get to sex."

"What's your attitude to sex?"

"Infrequently."

"Is that one word or two?"

If her sister could see her now, she'd fall about laughing at the ridiculous position she'd voluntarily put herself in... just to *'one up'* her. Liz also couldn't help noticing that her neighbours on all three sides were in their own gardens and another 27 reasons for not yelling out "Shagger!" at the top of her voice sprang to mind.

Impatiently, she drew in a deep breath. The intoxicating blend of roses, jasmine, and lavender filled her nose and lungs. The garden was so beautiful at this time of year. A fragrant frenzy of sweet and floral notes.

She relaxed a little.

I mean, what's the likelihood that the pup would even know its name? She could probably yell anything and it would ignore her just the same.

As the words reverberated around in her head, she found herself singing the two syllables and the awful realisation that the sing-songy way we call out in two pitches means loudly singing Shhaaaa - grrrr, Shhaaaa - grrr, Shhaaaa - grrr.

It would've been so much easier to call the dog Spot. She wondered vaguely how long "Out damn Spot" jokes would stay funny. Probably, funnier, than her current situation at least.

She'd known for years that they called her Macbeth when they thought she couldn't hear. She liked it, appreciating both the references and the affection because as nicknames go... she could just as easily have been called Witch 1, 2 or 3, or some other random female Shakespearean character.

She knew that Ray already thought of her mother and her sisters as the three witches from Macbeth. Early in their relationship he'd come into her mother's kitchen to see the three sisters arguing over a boiling pot on the stove. He quickly turned around and made an exit muttering, 'double, double, toil and trouble. Fire burn and cauldron bubble'. It was a difficult image to displace.

Anyway, maybe it would be more appropriate to call the dog Spot.

Just then, the dog appeared from under a nearby bush and ran into the house brushing against her legs and rendering the decision moot for the moment. Mental note to self: This will need addressing soon.

"Wait!..."

"Stop!..."

She called in vain. The dog took no notice and its muddy feet and body straight into the living room and jumped on the couch.

The pup may not live long enough for a name change, she thought.

As she chased the dog into the living room her eye was drawn to the mantelpiece and the "Get better soon" card her sister had sent her recently. She wasn't ill or anything, her sister just thought she could be a better human. In her sister's world, being a journalist for The Morning News was code for '*corporate sell-out*'. It was just another indication of how their sense of humour differed.

As she moved the dog into the kitchen and closed all the doors in a vain attempt to keep the dog in one room, she looked at the dishes from breakfast and instantly mentally erased them from her mind.

This was one of her super-powers. The ability to completely ignore things that were right in front of her.

She thought about how she was doing it with Ray lately. They were having problems and she really didn't want to deal with it. She was focusing more on work and they were spending less time together. She couldn't help but notice that their third '*7 year itch*' was coming up.

They had no kids, which seemed to be her fault, though Ray had never made a big deal about it. He focussed on his projects and had become absorbed in trying to get one of his ideas to work. Ray had so much of his identity wrapped up in turning one of his ideas into a success. Some kind of child replacement strategy maybe? She knew that it was a poor substitute for a family and was thankful that he never brought it up or complained about it.

Their lives had changed so much since they got married. Her late career change to journalism was mostly working out and on the whole she enjoyed it. Every job has parts that get up your nose. There are always some strange and objectionable colleagues in every workplace. The newspaper wasn't as bad as her experience with the public service. The level of entitlement, laziness, incompetence and ego had been breathtaking to witness and a soul-destroying price to pay for what the community gained.

| 5 |

Edward Andrews

Fraud, embezzlement and Charity

As Edward Andrews made his entrance into the Grand Ballroom he could feel the scrutinising gaze of a thousand pairs of eyes. The huge crystal chandeliers were subtly reflected in the marble floors, the extravagant jewellery and the highly polished instruments of the orchestra. He smiled confidently as he surveyed the room. This year's annual charity fundraiser was absolutely dripping with opulence and affluence.

Everywhere he looked there were beautiful women in fabulous gowns, and glittering jewellery. Haute couture. Haute coiffure. Haute Joaillerie. Haute Parfumerie de niche. Haute Horlogerie. Haute everything.

He loved being the host of his own black tie gala. His team looked after every aspect of the event and he just had to turn up and revel in the glory of it all. He absolutely enjoyed the way it made people suck up to him. Their fawning, gushing, overflowing compliments. These people were so phoney, so eager to be in his good books, so full of hot air, crap and money.

He'd always run these events the same way. An extravagant open bar, celebrity appearances and staggering giveaways and auction items. This year the main auction item was an 80 day trip round the world. It had attracted a lot of interest on local news and radio feeding the common people's fascination with the excesses of the rich and famous.

He glanced at his watch. Ten minutes before his speech. His gaze lingered and admired his rose gold Patek Philippe Calatrava. It was his favourite. Such a classic timepiece. His watch collection contained several vintage Patek Philippe's which he liked for formal occasions but tended to wear his Jaeger-LeCoultre Master Ultra Thin for every day. He really liked how the Calatrava looked beside his lapis lazuli cufflinks, tie pin and signet ring, all surrounded in gold. The rose gold and blue of the lapis lazuli perfectly matched his skin tan, tones and eyes, or so he'd been told.

His speech was timed to coincide with the initial wave of alcoholic euphoria that was achieved after 45 minutes of an open bar.

Looking around the room, he watched the youngest generation of aspiring entrepreneurs and socialites scramble for opportunities to climb the social ladder by securing a lucrative deal or landing a coveted invitation. What a bunch of losers!

It seemed so long since he'd been one of them. He pretended to himself that he'd never been one of them.

Two flawless young women dressed in stunning gowns and diamond necklaces drew his attention as they danced seductively towards him. They turned on their most appealing smiles and poses as they tried to lure him in. He smiled back at them, beckoning towards his PA whispering, "Invite those two to the after party upstairs."

His PA nodded, knowingly.

He patted the copy of his speech in the pocket of his dinner jacket reassuringly. He'd be reading it from the teleprompter but always liked having a physical copy at his fingertips, just in case. Experience had shown that technology does fail from time to time.

His title in the charity was founder and president which included a base salary of one million dollars a year. The charity's mission changed from year to year as choosing new directions meant that they could focus on different people, businesses and sponsors rather than fleece the same ones every year. He liked being called the president.

This year it was all about the homeless.

He didn't really care for the homeless or even care about them really. They were just a means to an end. He mostly picked something topical as this meant mainstream news did a lot of his advertising for him, describing and presenting the issues. If they made a Four Corners or 60 Minutes show about it, he knew he was onto a winner.

Last year the focus had been on medical research. 12 million dollars had been raised and just over 1.5 million was actually passed on to fund research. That'd been a good year. He'd squirrelled away nearly 10 million dollars from that and all legally so his team tells him. Those stupid socialite types could barely remember who or what they gave money to last year. They only thought about being seen and looking good.

Each event meant finding a new gown, new shoes, getting hair done, makeup, manicures, tanning, massages and some strategic shaving. The life of a socialite. What a bunch of complete airheads. He despised them. Even more than he despised the homeless and needy.

Each year he watched socialites with more money than sense dress up in tens of thousands of dollars worth of gowns, shoes and makeup, buy a table or a seat for tens of thousands more to come along and play the *'I'm a better person than you because I gave or spent more money than you did'* game.

His PA indicated it was time to move to the main stage and two large men in dinner suits cleared the way, guiding him to the steps beside the stage. He took out his paper copy of the speech ready to arrange it on the podium. Taking a deep breath and fixing his confident smile, he waited calmly for the MC to introduce him.

A sparkly dressed MC declared in a strong, clear announcer voice. "Ladies and Gentlemen... honoured guests, please help me welcome our host for this evening. Ladies and Gentlemen, please give a warm welcome to our generous benefactor, the founder and president Mr Edward Andrews."

He stepped forward and waited patiently until the applause died down.

"Ladies and gentlemen, distinguished guests, fellow philanthropists...

Welcome to this magnificent evening, a night dedicated to a cause close to all our hearts. As President of this fantastic charity, this incredible organisation, I stand before you humbled but filled with immense pride and gratitude."

"We are gathered here tonight, not just for exquisite food and elegant company, but for a purpose far greater. Raising vital funds that will change countless lives. Every dollar you contribute holds the power to transform lives, giving people hope, opportunities, and a chance to thrive. We are architects of a better tomorrow, builders of hope, and an unwavering force for good."

"Some incredible auction items have been donated and I look forward to seeing your generosity and competitive natures emerge."

He looked around the room and smiled warmly.

"I'm sure there'll be a lot of interest in that once-in-a-lifetime trip to the Galapagos Islands in the footsteps of Charles Darwin and the Beagle. I like the sound of that one myself."

"I also like the idea of a private concert by a well-known symphony orchestra."

He looked knowingly in the direction of the orchestra conductor, who returned the look with an inclining bow.

"So many amazing items and of course, a lot of surprises."

"You can view the auction items to my right. Please check out what is available and set your heart on something. This is also where you'll find many of our celebrity guests. Make yourself known to them and they'll be delighted to take a selfie with you as you check out what's in the auction. Think of the potential bragging rights if you get a selfie with all of them."

He smiled broadly, scanning the room. They were with him. He moved in for the hard sell.

"Remember, the future we envision isn't just possible, it's within reach. Let's make it a reality, together. Let's make it our crowning achievement."

"I urge you to open your hearts, wallets and purses tonight. Please raise your glasses and let your generosity flow like the Dom Perignon champagne at every table."

"Thank you and let the fun and the fundraising begin! Enjoy!"

As he soaked up the warmth of the applause, he smiled the genuine, sincere smile he'd practised so carefully. Savouring the affection of the crowd, he waved, smiled and thought. "Suckers". Waving a final time at the adoring sycophants as he left the podium.

Well, that's my official bit done. I wonder how my PA got on with those two young hotties. They looked like they might be up for anything.

He spotted an elderly woman dripping in diamonds making a beeline for him gushing compliments.

"It's such a wonderful night Edward, you really have outdone yourself... and you look so handsome."

He studied the woman closely. She was about 30 years older than him and dressed in a glittering gown and swathed in sparkling jewels.

He smiled graciously and said, "Glad you're enjoying yourself Madeleine. Is your husband here tonight?"

"Yes, he's talking about boring stuff I don't care about with some Senators. Tonight, I'm just a girl that wants to have fun", she said giggling girlishly.

"Well Madeleine, let's see what we can do about that."

"Allow me to introduce you to our celebrities. Is there anyone you would like to meet?"

"Are there any film people? Any sports people?", she asked hopefully.

"There certainly is. Now let's see who we can find."

He walked her to a table surrounded by a small, excited crowd. They parted as he walked closer revealing four of the celebrities. He couldn't remember any of their names, he just knew they were sports people and entirely mercenary. He didn't mind that. Even understood it. He was just amused by the hypocrisy. These hypocrites had learnt to show care and compassion about anything if they were paid enough and they negotiated their fees ruthlessly. He sort of liked it.

He looked at the small elderly woman at his elbow. Her eyes were like saucers. She knew who they were and was getting the full effect.

He turned to her and said, "Excuse me Madeleine but I have other people to attend to. I hope you have a great night".

Gently pushing her forward he said, "This is Madeleine. Take good care of her."

As he walked away, he thought about his unfinished business with Madeleine's husband. He'd run up considerable debts at one of his clubs and was now in a nice flexible position which he planned taking advantage of very soon. Her husband was a very senior official at APRA, The Australian Prudential Regulation Authority and one of the key signatures he needed to finalise his purchase of a bank.

He was feeling confident that he had the first signature in the bag. So far, Madeleine's husband had been the easiest of the four to manipulate with gambling, sex and alcohol. The idea of doing the deal completely legally and without applying pressure had never occurred to him. He naturally assumed he'd need leverage.

The other 3 signatures he needed were more complicated. One was a health nut and a lay preacher with no obvious vices. One was near retirement and already had a large stock and property portfolio. Again no obvious vices or blackmailable past. The final one was a wealthy, unmarried bachelor. He'd sounded the most promising. There must be some reason why he chose the single life. Secretly gay? Asexual? His people had found no reason so far that could be exploited. They would have to keep digging.

The irony wasn't lost on him. That description could apply to him as well. He was wealthy and unmarried. Was there a reason he had never married?

Of course there was.

His mother had told him not to get married. She'd understood him, worked him out. In her opinion he'd be better off with a mistress and a housekeeper. She'd been right. A wife would've been too intrusive into his life. Maybe this guy was the same. It seemed unlikely but possible.

He really liked the way his life was at the moment. He was a well-respected businessman running legal and illegal businesses. He ran this charity. He held a significant property portfolio. He had his long-term mistresses.

He looked around the room. With all these suckers and their money, life would continue to be good. He briefly wondered if his PA had organised those two girls to attend his after party?

Time to go and work the room. Time to talk bullshit and hand out compliments to these meticulously dressed and manicured social butterflies that reek of piles of money.

He noticed a couple hovering nearby. He could see that they wanted to approach and talk with him but were hesitant, so he walked up to them and greeted them warmly.

“Are you having a good night?”

“Absolutely Mr Andrews. My name is Drake. Alexander Drake”, extending his hand, “and this is my daughter Cynthia.”

“Delighted to meet you both.” Edward Andrews shook Alexander Drake’s outstretched hand warmly then turned to take Cynthia’s hand making an elegant display of kissing her hand.

“Cynthia, that fragrance you're wearing is captivating, truly a delight”, Edward Andrews purred, “The notes are intriguing. Is there a story behind it?”

“Absolutely”, she gushed enthusiastically.

"For my 21st birthday, Daddy arranged for me to go to Paris to visit a famous perfumer who created it just for me. She squeezed her father affectionately. The notes are... she quoted almost mechanically, ‘A complex interplay of bergamot, rose absolute, and oud’, Isn’t it beautiful?"

"Delightful. You are one lucky girl. I’ve an interest in perfumery myself. Perhaps you could tell me more about it sometime?"

"I'd be delighted. Over a glass of champagne, perhaps?" Cynthia suggested, forgetting her father’s presence for a moment.

He smiled, excused himself and moved on. The words ‘Note to self. Nail her later.’ echoing in his head.

To his left, a group of elegantly dressed women were deep in conversation dropping haute couture names like litter. Jimmy Choo, Christian Louboutin, Chanel, Dior. At the mention of each name he could see the thrill they evoked. They loved those names more than fanboys love Tesla, Apple and Marvel.

To his right, another group of gorgeously dressed women were discussing and comparing jewellery. Again, dropping names like they were lobbing grenades. 57 facets of Cartier, Van Cleef mingled with the carat, cut, clarity and colour of Tiffany and the Cabochon style.

He stopped briefly at each group, complimenting the first on their magnificent gowns and the second on their stunning jewellery. He engaged the elite with practised charm, his conversations sprinkled with references to exclusive clubs and philanthropic endeavours. This created the desired effect and he watched their egos swell and inflate as they absorbed the flattery.

Unfortunately knowing this stuff was part of the social lubrication. To notice and compliment the women on their gown, jewels, shoes and perfume was part of the glue that kept their fragile egos alive.

He always made sure to drop a seed into each conversation to encourage them to really overspend, over donate or compete financially.

He usually targeted the older women who wanted the spotlight back on them now their looks and vitality had faded. If he could build on the sense of vanity, rivalry and one upmanship that already existed it could add millions and it would all go straight to him. They would be his millions.

Will you be this year's top donor and earn that special place in all our hearts?

Will you be the champion of philanthropy?

Will you be my hero?

| 6 |

Sunday at the pub

Sunday Afternoon

As usual on Sunday afternoons, Ray headed off to spend the afternoon with his friend Gabe. The beautiful Gabriel. He was one of God's gifts to women. Ray had seen the photos of Gabe's christening at his parent's house. He was an impossibly angelic looking child and he could see why his parents had named him Gabriel.

Before he'd settled down with his not quite as beautiful wife, it was one of his favourite chat up lines "Would you like the gift of the Gab?" It usually got a smile at least.

Gabe and his wife Molly made a wonderful couple. They really liked each other. It wasn't a lust-fuelled romance but more a case of two old souls that had found themselves again.

As far as he knew, they were one of those rare couples that were genuinely content. They lived and worked together nearly continuously and he'd never seen a cross word between them, they deeply cared for each other. They each thought that the other was wonderful and they were lucky to have them.

Ray and Gabe would catch up most Sunday afternoons at their local pub. They'd been doing it for years. They never got rolling drunk, just a bit merry and enjoyed each other's company immensely.

Sometimes they were joined by their wives but not today. It depended on what was on. All four of them had played in bands when they were younger and still enjoyed good music. The Sunday sessions at the pub were well established and they had their favourites of the bands that came through. Both wives liked to dance and so did the husbands after about beer number three.

As Ray walked in he could see Gabe off in the corner chatting with another local, whose name he couldn't quite remember. The band wasn't due to start for another hour or so but he could hear them starting to tune up next door as a small group of older women started to dance to their soundcheck. It was a tepid, minimal movement sort of dancing. Nearly like they had an allergy to music, or perhaps they were saving their energy. He wasn't sure. Best not to dwell on that, he thought.

He waved to Gabe and conducted an elaborate hand waving semaphore, to see if he wanted a drink, worked out that he didn't and so he went to the bar and got himself one.

As he walked over to Gabe, he just heard the tail end of the conversation... the local, whose name he couldn't remember, was saying, "The answer to this global warming thing seems obvious. Just get everyone to turn their air conditioning units around the other way and cool the world down to whatever temperature you like."

Gabe nodded diplomatically and said, "You could be right, John" and turned to Ray.

"How are ya Ray?" raising his glass.

"Good. Good. Solving the world's problems already, you two. I hope you left some for me to solve too", said Ray smiling.

They all laughed. They were all looking forward to an afternoon of stories, jokes and generally talking crap.

"So, how's the new pup?" Gabe asked.

"Liz has named him '*Shagger*' after he showed affection for my leg. I hope we can get him out of that habit quickly. Apart from that, he seems like a lively little thing."

Just then, the environmental activist with the air conditioning plan was accosted by another old regular.

"You know that expression, mutton dressed as lamb?"

"Yeh."

"So mutton is an old lamb, right?"

"Yeh."

"So what's old mutton called?"

"I don't know, Why?"

"I think your dates just arrived."

Environmental solutions man took a good-natured swipe at him as he wandered off.

"Cheeky bugger. Have you seen his girlfriend?

Actually, I got a new dog six months ago and he never comes to me or does anything I say. It's not that he doesn't understand me, he just doesn't listen. I told my ex-wife and she said it'd restored her faith in karma."

They all laughed. They'd heard it before. A few times.

The joke telling was getting started early today.

Good thought Ray, he liked that.

| 7 |

Angie's motivation

One year earlier

Angela Murray slowed her car to a crawl as she entered her apartment's parking garage. Turning into her personal space the car's headlights lit up on a still figure huddled at the back of her parking spot.

Braking to a stop, she tried to work out what to do. The figure suddenly shivered, flexed and turned towards the headlights.

WTF?

It took her a moment to recognise who it was.

It was Cassie... and she'd been badly beaten. Her eyes and face were swollen and covered in streaks of tears and blood.

My God!

She'd met Cassie 8 or 9 years ago when she first went to university and they shared a room. Cassie got her the job at the club.

Without turning off the engine, she released her seat belt, leapt from the car and rushed to the broken figure, "Cassie what's happened? What's going on?"

Cassie peered up at her through swollen eyes, "Angie?"

The words were barely audible. She looked like a mess. Black eyes, split lip. Blood caked around her face.

"Angie, I didn't know what to do? I didn't know where else to go. " She burst into tears, "Help me."

"Who did this?", Angie demanded, bending down to comfort her.

"Pleeeease... don't ask me that."

"Can you walk? Do you need an ambulance? Angie asked, unsure what to do."

"Let me get you to the back of the car and let's see what we're dealing with."

Angie tried to help Cassie to her feet but it was immediately obvious that this was causing her considerable pain.

"Let's get you back down", laying her back on the cold concrete. "Do you think you have any broken bones?"

"I don't know", she moaned, "My left leg and right arm don't seem right. They both hurt a lot... and my ribs."

Can you sit up a bit?

"Cassie, I just want to work out what we're dealing with, so I'm going to open your jacket."

As Angie began to open her jacket, Cassie let out a muffled cry and writhed in pain. The damage to her right arm was clear. Her wrist was dislocated, maybe broken. It wasn't supposed to point in that direction. She'd definitely need to go to the hospital.

"This is serious Cassie. I think I should call an ambulance."

"I'm scared Angie. Really scared. She's a psycho."

"She said I'd taken one of her clients. I didn't know. He picked me. He asked for me. Isn't that how it works?"

"Who?" Angie tried again.

"I only know her as *'Glitch'*. I don't know her real name."

"When I left work she was waiting for me. She decked me with the first punch and I just curled up into the smallest ball I could until she stopped kicking me. It seemed to last forever. She was yelling stuff at me all the way through and I got the message. It's time for me to leave."

"Yes, you do. You need to go to the hospital. You really do."

"But what about my son?"

"You have a son now? Wow! Can we call someone to look after him? Where is he now?"

"At my cousins. He's already got two kids."

This was the moment when Angie had her epiphany. She realised that many of the women that do this work are far more vulnerable than she realised. Not all but there are some. Same with drugs, alcohol and mental health issues. Not all but some.

For these women, if the wheels come off their life for any reason, they have no safety net to catch them. People like Cassie. Someone just trying to raise her kid.

A safety net would be a good thing to have. Something to catch them when they fall. Rock bottom could be a net.

A small flame flickered into life inside her.

She drove Cassie to the hospital and rang her cousin and explained that Cassie was in the hospital and he agreed to look after her son. He asked what had happened and if it had anything to do with work.

He said, "I know what she does for a living and I've been worried about her. She's told me some shocking stories. Is she involved in something bad?"

"I really don't know."

She recounted what had happened since she pulled into the car park.

"Should I let her parents know?"

"I don't know. I've never met them."

"They are a traditional conservative family. I don't think they'll cope very well if they find out."

"I'll leave that to you. I'll check on her each day and let you know how she is, if you like."

"Thanks, I appreciate that. We spent a lot of time together growing up and I know she has a good heart; I just wish she'd taken a different path."

Over the next week, Angie visited Cassie in the hospital and they got to know each other again. It'd been seven years since they'd lived together and they'd lost touch.

Cassie's life had changed since the arrival of her son. She became a single mother two years ago and things had been hard. Her son needed various medical treatments and even though they were mostly covered, not entirely. Money had been tight and she'd taken riskier work to get by.

As Cassie progressively opened up to Angie, she told her stories of violence, rape, police indifference and widespread discrimination from medical staff and church groups. This was very different to the world that Angie had experienced.

Like Angie, Cassie had needed money and agreed to sex work. It hadn't always gone well. The third time, the client had grown impatient with her and become violent.

Later, she got caught up in a police sting and a police officer demanded sex and money from her. The more Angie heard about her life and experiences, the more she realised how much they contrasted with her own.

She marvelled at the simple and basic things she should've thought about but hadn't, like whether the club she worked at was legal. She'd just assumed it must be but realised now that this was naive. There probably was a criminal side to the club.

A few google searches found that there were sex worker alliances in many countries and they were nearly all working towards the same goals.

The basic message seemed to be 'sex work is work'.

The aim was to get the world to see sex work from that perspective. As income generating work and not as criminal activity. If it's seen as work then all the usual workers' rights, protections and responsibilities would apply.

In many countries, the barrier is whether sex work is legal or not. If it's not legal, then the opportunities for abuse are broader. If it's legal, a sex worker has ways to make sure they get paid, have access to medical services and the police will help if violence is threatened.

The more she found out about the issues around the world, the stronger her resolve became to do something about it.

In countries where it's decriminalised it was typical to hear stories like 'I've never had to call the police but I know I can and if I did, they'd take me seriously.'

Contrast that with countries where it is still illegal. Angie had never thought about the problems it creates when a sex worker tries to apply for a bank loan, rent a home or gain access to medical care. These were real world practical, everyday issues.

During the week that Cassie was in hospital recovering, her family were contacted by the police because of some mandatory reporting of domestic violence requirements.

Unfortunately, this meant her family found out what she did, either from her cousin, the police or the hospital and disowned her. Her options for family support dried up and just before she was released from hospital she was evicted from her flat when someone tipped off her landlord who somehow thought he could be charged with running an illegal house, even though that wasn't how Cassie worked.

Cassie's parents were considering adopting her son by having her declared unfit through failure to provide basic needs and bringing her parental fitness into question.

Unfortunately, over the next year she got to know lots of tragic stories like this. The more stories and research she did, the angrier and more motivated she became.

After many nights of searching, she settled on two projects that resonated with her.

Firstly, Amnesty International with a well-documented history of recognising sex worker rights, developing policy and advocating for the adoption of those policies.

... and secondly, The Global Network of Sex Work Projects had similar aims with initial wins advocating to organisations like the United Nations for the adoption of the term sex work and sex worker being used to show that it is work.

These two organisations were targeting three core values and goals:

1. The acceptance of sex work as work.
2. Opposition to all forms of criminalisation and other legal oppression of sex work including sex workers, clients, third parties, families, partners and friends.
3. Supporting self-organisation and self-determination of sex workers.

With her legal training and her small experience with sex work, she could help people in their struggles. She could help her friend Cassie but how many more Cassies were out there.

This could bring a new purpose to her life. This could be her mission.

| 8 |

On the train

Monday Morning

The railway station was fairly busy and the raucous laughter of children echoed throughout the building as he joined the end of the smaller queue at the ticket counter. The competing aromas of freshly brewed coffee and freshly baked bread assaulted Ray's senses. He breathed in deeply. An olfactory overload. A pungent pageant. A malodorous medley... that didn't take long, he'd run out of alliterations already.

The well-dressed couple in front of him were signing something. As the clerk read it, he looked up at the older man, stood to attention and saluted.

The woman beside him rolled her eyes and said wearily. "Don't salute him." "He wasn't in the military. His name is Colin... not Colonel."

"Now then Carolina, he wasn't to know", said the older man, called Colin.

Ray had once dated a girl called Carolina and the words transported him back to the first time they went to dinner. She was sitting at the table looking beautiful and he could only see the top half of her or as he thought of it, North Carolina.

It was a terrible metaphor because it made him immediately think of South Carolina... and after that he just felt naughty. As he'd mused many times, it's a colossal mistake to underestimate the power of naughty. He had to stop himself from singing the James Taylor song… "In my mind I'm going to Carolina". That relationship, well… it hadn't worked out.

After getting his ticket he went in search of his platform and carriage. He ignored the freshly baked pastries, hot coffee and hard to understand train announcements as they wafted from the cafes, bakeries and speakers. The station was loud and busy and he jostled through the bustle until he reached his platform.

It looked like it was going to be full and he found a seat as he felt the train get underway. The station soon gave way to the cityscape and then vibrant green fields, dotted with grazing cattle and wildflowers. As the train settled into its cruising speed, he surveyed the carriage in his best Sherlock Holmes imitation. What can I deduce about the people around me?

The woman directly opposite was engrossed in a small hardback book. She was quite heavily rugged up, with a scarf, beanie and mittens. I didn't think it was that cold, he thought. Is that significant? As he watched, she turned a page and coughed.

That's a deep cough, he thought. In fact, that didn't sound like a woman at all. Why'd he thought it was a woman? His eyes focussed on the book cover. "Blood, Sweat and Cheers - A surprising collection of cocktail recipes". OK, I have no idea what's going on there… I'll come back to her later.

The woman next to her appeared to be heavily spanxed. She was in her early forties and in near continuous motion as bits of her kept bulging impressively out from her outfit while she tried to equally unobtrusively squeeze them back in. It was an on-going battle and obviously one that she'd chosen willingly. Sometimes, it is reassuring to see that sort of mindless optimism and hopefulness. He usually enjoyed it and in the one and only book he'd written there was a chapter about it.

Next to the window was a large woman of nearly equal proportions in every direction. For the rest of the journey he would think of her as Square Peg. Square Peg must have been widely known in her local community for not fitting into the space normally provided for humans to sit. She must have had trouble fitting in a standard cinema or bus seat... or civic meeting, submarine or anywhere much. Do Sumo wrestlers have special chairs, he wondered?

As he looked at her, all the while suppressing the internal dialogue that wanted to start with, "I wonder what the fuck happened to her?" he tried to size her up as Sherlock might. One of Sherlock's party tricks was to guess height, weight and occupation. He studied her carefully. Hard to tell the height while she is sitting down and weight... hmmm.

He started trying to visualise how many 3kg bags of oranges she would be? It was hard to tell. Maybe it's better to try to calculate her volume. He tried to remember the formula. Something about circumference and pi. He grinned involuntarily. I bet there was a lot of pie involved to make that circumference.

His grin turned sheepish. Oh boy, that's lame.

As the train rattled on, he closed his eyes but found it impossible to drown out the conversation between the two people behind him. He couldn't see them and didn't want to look but he was sure he heard one of them declare that he knew nothing about Middle Eastern politics but somehow then went on to elaborate and pontificate on the theme for the next twenty minutes. I really must get some noise cancelling headphones, Ray thought.

His internal trialogue was discussing the various merits of just turning around and either yelling “Shut the fuck up you morons”, being violent towards them or practicing his meditations. At this stage there was no clear-cut winner, although there seemed to be a lot of internal support for both the yelling and the violence.

He tried once again to go to his happy place and conjured up that mental image of a happy veterinarian skipping down the hill, approaching the flock singing "What's a matter ewe?"

Ahh... that’s better, he thought. I think I’ll just stay here for a while.

| 9 |

Liz's new assignment

Monday Morning

Liz nervously sipped her coffee as she waited for her editor to return for their meeting. She didn't like her editor much. She was a bit '*pitbull in lipstick with a touch of sociopathy thrown in*'. The meeting should have started by now but the editor was nowhere to be seen. Olivia Clemens had become the editor after many years following fashion, politics and crime. In her style, she didn't just follow it, she stalked it. This led to a certain reputation.

Don't fuck with me!

Fear works to get things done but doesn't always bring loyalty. In a private poll held each year amongst the journalists, the editor had been the winner of the '*biggest rectum of the year*' competition each year since taking the editors role, beating the paper's owner, which had been new. As usual, in these things, no one ever said it to her and no trophy was presented, although there'd been recent speculation about a lifetime achievement award.

Liz liked the editor's assistant, Sue and they sometimes had lunch together or caught up for a drink or meal after work. Their friendship had started over Sue's brilliant way with words. The first time they met, Liz had gone to see the editor and asked Sue, "Is she in?".

"She's talking to her Irish friend again," said Sue with a smile.

"Irish friend? " asked Liz, confused.

"Yeh, His name is O'Shit", said Sue, "she's been saying his name over and over for at least an hour." "I really don't fancy interrupting. She doesn't sound happy with him".

Today, she waited patiently but nervously and they chatted amicably. The editor finally arrived, 20 minutes late in a cloud of foul language, loose papers and stale cigarette smoke. She didn't appear to be in a good mood at all.

I'll just let her settle down a bit, Liz thought.

A few minutes later Liz was hovering outside the editor's office trying not to be noticed, embracing her inner coward and praying to unspecified but definitely unatheistic gods that the meeting would be cancelled. As usual, appeals to deities seemed to be going to message bank.

"Okay Elizabeth, what did I want to see you about?" the editor asked rhetorically.

"That's right, you're going to be our mystery shopper", she answered herself.

Liz cringed at the use of her full name and said, "I don't quite understand what you want?"

"Oh, it's simple really. Mark had this idea about doing a series of articles about our advertisers with our journo's playing mystery shoppers. We can write advertorials about different industries and sell some advertising at the same time. I think the whole idea was based around him doing the Adult Services section but I've burst that bubble. The idea is okay but I'm not prepared to give the little shit the satisfaction. So, I want you to do that section. We'll run the articles in six or seven months, so there's good lead time. We'll need time to align the advertorials and features. "

"What exactly do you want? I don't know anything about this…", Liz's voice trailed away.

"I didn't think so," purred the editor in a superior tone, "That's what makes you perfect for it," adding, "You don't have to use their services... unless you want to."

"What do you want to know about it?" asked Liz resignedly.

"I want you to personalise it. Think about the things you don't know about adult services that your average punter wouldn't know either."

"Surely there would be someone better for this than me, Liz whined, "I am really uncomfortable with this".

"I know", the editor smiled wickedly and steamrolled on, "That's why I chose you. All the blokes wanted it but you can provide a perspective that none of them can."

Liz looked blankly while her mind tried to find some solid ground. "How? Where? I don't know where to start?"

"Same place as any other story. Are you a real journalist or not? What is the difference between a murder or sex scandal and this? Look, to get you started, I'll set up an interview with a spokesperson and advocate for a sex workers alliance that I met. She's agreed to be available for up to three hours if I pay her by the hour. I'll send her an outline of the articles and I think you'll find that she'll give you a completely different perspective."

"But…"

"Stop your whinging and get on with it. Now get out, I have other things to deal with." The editor finished the sentence with a finality that didn't invite further input.

With that, she bellowed something loud and objectionable at her assistant Sue but Liz wasn't listening as her mind was ín high gear trying to work out what to do.

As she walked back to her desk, her mind was reeling from the conversation. Can I do this? Should I quit? Refuse? How will we pay the mortgage? Oh God! What am I going to do? She returned to her desk to find Amanda from legal waiting for her, unusually wearing normal clothes and a strange expression.

"Sorry I'm late", Liz started, "but you know what she's like".

"Sure. Hi", Amanda said cheerfully. "Look, it's about that article on Dr George King that you wanted approved. Can't do it. I know it is begging for light relief but we have to be restrained. The problem line is...

'Researchers are still trying to piece together what happened after the terrible events when Dr George King, deaf to the near universal pleas to stop, doggedly pursued his curiosity and investigation into whether large mammals are ticklish.'

"So, you are absolutely sure that I can't say 'piece together what happened", Liz asked, smiling mischievously.

"Absolutely not", replied Amanda firmly, stifling a smirk.

"Scraping together a conclusion?" suggested Liz, looking innocently upwards.

Another firm head shake and "No" from Amanda.

Liz tried once more, "What about the madness of George King?"

"No puns please Liz, this is serious, dozens of people were traumatised," Amanda said trying to maintain her professional bearing.

"I know", said Liz dryly, "but why do I want to roll on the floor, laughing hysterically? Don't you think there's a humorous side to this?"

"Of course I do", said Amanda, "We've been falling about upstairs all morning, but you need to find some language that is respectful to a distinguished scientist and researcher."

"You sure you don't mean extinguished scientist and researcher? I wonder, do you have to be alive to get an Ig Nobel award?" Liz wondered rhetorically.

"Stop it", Amanda said, rolling her eyes.

"What about a Darwin award?", Liz chuckled, "Can we nominate him?"

Amanda's brow furrowed, "Now, that could make an interesting story."

| 10 |

On the plane

Monday Afternoon

The flight was getting rough.

Ray was working on a technique he'd read about for when you are feeling uncertain, think about the last thing that got you fired up and use it to put some fire in your belly to combat anxiety and distress.

He went straight back to the previous weekend when he was reading the Sunday papers. It was an article reporting that scientists had recently discovered that we share 99.99% of our DNA with politicians. Once again this kicked off an internal mental process filled with questions and outrage. How can this be? How do they know? Which scientists? All politicians? What about lawyers, public servants, umpires and parking meter attendants?

He was deep in thought and fuelling the fires of indignation when the passenger next to him asked how to spell the word *'testament'*. This shattered his concentration as the consequences of the question filtered through his consciousness.

"Are you writing a will?"

He immediately regretted the question and began desperate and silent appeals to any deity that would listen.

In spite of this, the man proceeded.

He opened his wallet and got out a battered photo. “These are my adult children from my first marriage as babies. I carry it around to remind me that I used to love them.”

He smiled thinly. “It’s a joke... but at moments like this, I realise that I still love them very much. No matter how much they stress me out.”

Ray introduced himself and found his fellow traveller was called Richard. Richard began to speak but fell silent as the plane rattled a bit more... and then dropped for a few seconds. They both gripped their seats through a variety of methods even more tightly.

Richard continued rapidly.

“My father taught it to me. He pointed out to me when I was about to become a parent that if you are in your teens and beyond and your parents have a picture of you as a baby in their main living space and see it every day... it means you’ve been a handful! At times they’ve needed the reminder... to look into your eyes as a child.”

Ray knew he wasn’t the favourite child. In desperate times, he was fairly sure that if his father had to pick which child he saved, it wasn't going to be him. He’d realised this early on and felt that he could imagine the general climate and conversation as the biblical Isaac and his father Abraham walked back down the mountain, just after Abraham had tried to kill him.

“It's nothing personal Isaac, God told me to do it. Turns out, it was just a test. You have to laugh... ehh?”

His Mum used to say that his father collected bottles, like his grandfather. It was a long time before he realised that this was code. His dad collected bottles. It's better than saying alcoholic... A bit like his aunt who always said she was five foot twelve... not 6 foot.

The only thing that had really stuck with him was more an observation than wisdom. Playing charades is the worst time to have a heart attack.

The plane settled a bit... and they got chatting.

Well... Richard continued to unburden and Ray continued to listen.

10 years ago as the crow flies, Richard had become step-father to two other kids and had come to think of himself as Faux-Pa. He developed a view, reinforced over many years, that having an adopted family is like running a small, badly funded correction facility. With your own kids, there is a certain *'Stockholm Syndrome'* aspect. You are captured by your kids by being completely in love with them.

Ray had been nodding in that convincing way he'd learnt to do with his wife and mother-in-law. It must be nearly time to nod and hmmm agreeably again. He did.

Richard continued talking.

It usually worked and it had again.

Richard was saying, "Like many parents, he went to sleep nearly every night reviewing his day and wondering whether any of his actions or decisions were valid, heartless or likely to cause long term psychological damage. He never really knew the answer to that question."

He'd remarried since then but eventually realised that while his new wife had passionately believed in no sex before marriage, he'd been surprised to find out and reluctantly accept that she didn't believe in it after marriage either. In a way he felt like he'd been conned. Society and the media were probably to blame... but as so many come to realise, it isn't easy to hold them accountable.

So instead, he travelled a lot for work. This always seemed like such a good idea until moments like this, when he found himself telling his life story to a complete stranger who is nearly as terrified as himself but without the compulsion to speak continuously. Probably something to do with being a salesman.

The plane eventually landed safely and as their heart rates and social boundaries returned to normal, Ray asked out of politeness, where Richard was heading next.

As it turned out, they were both staying in the same part of town and so his new friend offered Ray a lift, partly as a way of thanking him for listening while he was having his existential crisis.

His new friend went to organise a rental car while Ray waited in the food court. It was full. Surprisingly, he'd taken one of the last available tables. All the different cuisines were a wonderful assault on his senses. The curries and spices, the grilled meats and seafood, the pizzas and coffee. He wiped his mouth just to be sure he wasn't drooling. Those tantalising tastes. A smorgasbord of smells. He loved the idea of food courts and the slightly agonising decision-making process it forces on you as at this stage, he wanted it all. As he looked around, he noticed the food court was full of people looking around at all the other people. This is odd, he thought, as his amateur detective genes kicked in again.

He began to divide the diners into groups and categories. The single diners. The pairs. These were further subdivided into couples and friends or colleagues. Then there were the young families. He could see five young families close by. Each had a small child in some sort of vehicle or contraption. As he watched, he noticed that in each setting, one of the two adults was in constant movement. They were directing the scene while the partner looked on. The look on each immobile partner's face was the same, like a trapped frightened animal.

"How the fuck did I get here? I just went out for a few drinks with my mates."

After collecting the car, they stowed their luggage and got in.

Driving away, Ray asked Richard, "Where are you travelling from and to?"

Richard said, "I'm coming back from Africa."

"Wow, that must have been great. I suppose you always get the same first question. Did they know it's Christmas?"

Richard laughed in that *'polite'* way. People often did at Ray's jokes.

As Richard pulled out into traffic, he accelerated breathtakingly and with not enough looking in mirrors for Ray's liking. It turned out that he was one of those people who drove recklessly while declaring *'Jesus is my co-pilot and airbag'*.

"Yeah, but what about me? Is he mine too?" squeaked Ray.

"He could be if you let him", said Richard and winked.

Oh shit... a religious nut! Why hadn't he mentioned that before?

As they rushed past cars at uncomfortable, mortality invoking speeds, Ray asked himself the question again. What did he really think about all this religion stuff? Lots of people seemed to have strong opinions about it, so he probably should have too. Liz certainly did. At times he wondered whether she really believed in her atheism or just really enjoyed the argumentative side of it. After a few moments of soul searching, he realised that he was still somewhere between blah and meh.

When he first learned about religion, some religious types from a nearby theological college visited his primary school and talked about Jesus using a ventriloquist bible. He'd found it confusing when they talked about letting Jesus into your heart as he'd only recently learnt about the heart, the brain, the lungs and other organs and had trouble visualising how inviting Jesus into this thing that pumps blood around his body did anything or even quite how you did it? Does he enter through one of the main valves?

He wondered if it was like the *'Santa Claus coming down the chimney story'*? How does he get to be so small and didn't Jesus die a long time ago? He was sure they'd mentioned that too. It was a confusing time. He'd heard that a lot of people in America were religious and if that was true, he couldn't understand why the first lady wasn't called Eve?

That year he and his sister had put duct tape over the chimney cap protector and checked after Christmas. It'd not been moved. Santa Claus didn't enter the chimney through the normal rules of physical science. This seemed to lend some credence to the magic qualities of Santa although it got more confusing the following year when the chimney was demolished in a renovation and he still delivered presents. Magic indeed.

The trip was largely uneventful apart from one amusing part when they followed a futuristic looking car that had the full sports pack. On the aerodynamic bit on the rear of the car was a sticker saying, *'Harry kills Voldemort in the end'*. Ray thought the owner was a genius and wished he'd thought of it.

Eventually, Richard dropped him off at his hotel and he was surprised to say the least, but quickly realised that the mistake was his own fault. He had in all innocence asked a colleague if he knew of a *'half decent'* hotel in the town and The Grand Hotel had been recommended as *'half decent'*. It was confirmed by a helpful man waiting in line at the food hall. In fact, he assured him that it was *'half decent'* and pointed enthusiastically in the general direction.

In hindsight, neither of them had elaborated which half was which, preferring to leave that to his own process of discovery. From the outside, he wasn't sure, but he was hoping that the half that was decent was structural.

| 11 |

Angie's request

Three weeks ago

The large bedroom was filled with hints of leather, sandalwood, and freshly laundered linens, infused with a hint of expensive perfumes. They created a sophisticated, masculine scent and an atmosphere of quiet refinement and luxury.

Edward Andrews stood barefoot on the soft, plush carpet that muffled the sounds of the outside world. He was dressing slowly, his eyes locked on his companion, Angie, perched on the edge of the bed, gazing up at him.

"There's something I've been thinking about," Angie began, her fingers trailing along the contours of his arm. "I think we could do something to help the girls."

"What do you mean?", his words tinged with caution.

Angie's smile widened as she leaned in closer, her warm breath against his skin. "We could start an alliance, to fight for the rights of all the girls and help protect each other," she whispered seductively.

"That's a noble idea, Angie," he said, forcing a smile, his hand gently stroking her cheek, "But I'm not sure it's practical. These girls are scattered, isolated. They don't have the resources or the know-how to organise themselves."

"That's where we could come in," she retorted, her eyes maintaining a playful defiance. "We have the means, the connections, the influence. We could help them find their voice," her lips brushing against his ear.

As he finished dressing, he said, noncommittally, "I'll give it some thought."

She seemed to take this as encouragement and smiled back at him gratefully.

He left her to finish dressing and returned to his office on the 24th floor.

Edward Andrews lived in the top two floors of the 51 story building he owned. Officially his company Edward Andrews and Associates owned it but he was the CEO. The only way to access the top two floors was from the 24th floor where he kept his office. He considered this good security and a very deliberate separation of work and play, rarely taking anyone to his private space but there were some exceptions. He ordered a Geisha Coffee and sat in his favourite *'Thinking'* chair, an original Eames lounge with ottoman and stared out the large, tinted window at the busy city below.

He considered himself a wealthy and influential businessman who deserved luxuries in his life. He owned one of the largest buildings in the city and many other businesses. Some were legitimate and some were not. He enjoyed owning his clubs. They were very useful for impressing clients. It always surprised him how many deals could be influenced by taking a client or customer to one of his clubs. Giving them access to expensive alcohol, party drugs and sex workers had enabled him to build his empire to the scale it was. It had become so ingrained now that he expected it. Demanded it. Beautiful women, luxurious food and drink and lots of money, influence and power.

He kept his three favourite sex workers on retainers and at least once a month he'd try any interesting newcomers that caught his eye.

That's how he'd met Angie 3 years ago. He'd noticed her working in one of his clubs as a waitress. They'd developed a good relationship, skewed as it was by the financial transaction but she was intelligent, empathetic, sexually skilled and willing. It was a powerful combination. He had watched her many times move between characters, hiding her own personality in the ebb and flow of the sex play. She had impressive natural acting skills.

One of the things he liked about her was that she could cut straight to the heart of a matter. Her lawyer training probably. He'd liked that... previously. This recent request was skilfully framed in language that showed these sex workers were actually humans and that basic human rights, like the prevention of exploitation, fair pay, protection from violence were all reasonable things to ask for.

It just wasn't how he thought about it or had ever thought about it or wanted to think about it. He liked the exploitation. To his way of thinking, the girls wouldn't do some of the work if they weren't capable of being exploited. They all had some flaw or deficiency that allowed them to cross that line that made the work acceptable.

Isn't exploitation a basic business principle? Nearly always, the person that is paying is exploiting the person they are paying. As far as he knew this is how things had always been. One of the keys to being good at business is to know how to exploit a person or situation. This is one of the ways that you make money. The idea of helping people to avoid the exploitation he was profiting from seemed like a mad idea. Completely mad.

He certainly didn't think of the girls that worked for him as normal humans.

His initial shock was now turning to rage as he replayed the scene over and over in his mind. She would have to be stopped. He decided in the Machiavellian spirit that she would have to go. It was a shame, in many ways, as he'd enjoyed her very much. Maybe it was just that he only liked her when she didn't have opinions and requests. One moment he really enjoyed her and the next he had decided that she would have to go.

An old Kenneth Williams quote sprang into his mind. "She doesn't know it yet, but she's for the chop." It really was just a switch in his mind.

He'd once been introduced to a loathsome reptile of a man who knew how to solve human problems. He explained that sometimes the only solution to human problems is to remove the human. He talked about three people who did this type of work. "There's one who is at the absolute peak. He may be the best in the world and I tell you this for nothing, cause these guys aren't like hiring a plumber. You don't want a hitman as an enemy, especially one that's good at making accidents happen. Now I don't know whether you ever need any services like that but let me know if you ever do. I can steer you right."

He looked up the loathsome reptile's number and rang him.

"Do you remember we once talked about solving human problems?

"Yes", came a cautious reply.

"How does it work?"

The loathsome reptile relaxed. He was on familiar territory now. "Well, I'll make a call and if he's interested, he'll contact you. To get ready for his contact you'll need to buy a burner phone with a pre-paid or anonymous SIM card and install Signal on it. Signal provides end-to-end encryption. Pick and connect to a VPN provider before using Signal to take the call. This method uses two layers of end-to-end encryption which makes any conversation very hard to be intercepted by anyone."

Edward Andrews began to make arrangements.

| 12 |

Liz's story

The Past

Biblical and Shakespearean threads ran deeply through Liz's life and family. Her cousin became pregnant in her teens and ran off with a carpenter called Joseph. Her brother Stephen was stoned and her mother still referred to her father running off, as the parting of the red C.

The family had used very Christian names in earlier times and the generation of her great-grandparents had children with names like Faith, Hope and Joy. Unfortunately, they'd not really considered how it would affect future generations. Her mother had rung her one morning, very upset, to tell her that it was a sad day as the family had to report that Faith had died today. It seemed extra sad as Hope and Joy had died the year before.

The family moved away from those old-fashioned names but still liked giving siblings names that share a common theme. Liz's mum and sisters were April, May and June. June had named her kids Pearl and Ruby while April went for the more nature based

Sky, Blossom and Willow. Liz thought she should be grateful. Her mum just liked the royal family.

In her twenties, Liz had written a successful book that became '*The Procrastinator*' series. '*A procrastinator tries to diet and exercise*'. This was the initial hit. She followed up with the less successful, '*A procrastinator tries again*', then the even less successful '*A procrastinator has another go*' and finally the disastrous '*A procrastinator considers giving up*'. After those three less than stellar performances she'd been dropped by her publisher and forced to consider a new career.

Journalism had seemed a natural career option as writing whole books was just too much work and it messes with your head. She knew that she'd always write and considered writing a book about her family.

Her great-grandfather and his siblings, inspired by the Wright brothers, saw themselves as early pioneers of human flight. Of course, in the family they were known affectionately as Thud, Splat and Oh Dear.

Surely, she could get a story out of that. But was it a whole book? Maybe it was just a series of short stories.

Her great-grandfather had been a country doctor in the era when cars were still a novelty and doctors still visited patients in their homes. Her mother used to say that in those times in small country towns and villages, people tended to die of things that the local doctor could spell or at least where the doctor and coroner could agree on the spelling. There was charm in a lot of the family stories and that one had always tickled her.

Liz's first serious boyfriend was Todd, the brother of her friend Sarah from school. He was a year older and played in one of the school rock bands. Sarah and Todd encouraged her into playing music and she started on the drums. In her final year of high school Sarah and Liz formed an all-girl band at school with Molly on vocals and Jill on Bass. They performed at school assemblies and then the local battle of the bands challenge.

Todd, Sarah and Liz liked a lot of the same things. They shared the love of music. Liz loved the upcoming bands like Nirvana, Soundgarden, Pearl Jam, Alice in Chains and Hole. They also liked the grunge look. Doc Martens, flannel shirts and ripped jeans were their uniform.

For a while life settled into a comfortable routine. They would all meet up and go to Blockbuster video and get a movie for the night and settle in at one of their houses.

They could spend a long time in the video store as they just loved their movies.

The same thing happened at the CD shop. Hours could be spent exploring new music. In those days you could ask to hear some music and then go to a special area and listen to it through the headphones supplied.

The high school band became 'The Braidsmides', named after an event at a family wedding when Uncle Mortified had got uncertainly to his feet and declared loudly and confidently '*A toast to the Braidsmides*'. It seemed like a good band name.

They played in local bars and parties in the years after school.

The band became the focus of her friend group for the next few years.

They were just a bunch of girls that had grown on a diet of Disney animation movies and Kylie Minogue and were now into grunge and some punk.

It was an exciting time in the Disney world as classics like The little mermaid, Aladdin, Beauty and the beast and the Lion King all came out during that time.

When Ray had been cleaning up the spare room he'd come across some of her old school books and mementos from that time. There'd been a set list for one of their early gigs.

She looked at it proudly. They'd kicked ass. She'd forgotten about the grungy Disney stuff.

She stopped for a moment caught in the flood of memories. The simple fun. There was only her and Molly left now. She still missed Sarah deeply. Sometimes life can be so unfair. She'd always remember fondly the year they spent travelling. What a year! Her first real taste of freedom.

Jill was Jill and it was hard to deny that she'd done it to herself. Sad. It's hard to influence someone who is determined to self-destruct. She could remember some amazing nights and good gigs. In those days they all drank more heavily and often had what they called '*Paradoxical Nights*', meaning it was both a night they would never forget and a night they could hardly remember. She'd considered trying to write a movie script with the tagline '*A night she could hardly remember turned out to be a night she would never forget*'.

Another half-started project.

Thinking about half finished writing projects brought back memories of trying to rework '*Alice's Adventures in Wonderland*' into '*Alice's Adventures in Van Diemen's Land*' by making her trip down the rabbit hole as a parallel for transportation of convicts from England. The strange characters that she meets would be local people and animals.

She'd spent a summer on it and had gotten to know the original story pretty well as she tried to assign different roles to new characters. Some were easier than others. A large caterpillar sitting on a mushroom smoking a hookah. Which Tasmanian animal most closely resembles that? She lost a lot of time trying to work out something that made sense and couldn't think of a way to do it. The truth was, Alice's Adventures in Wonderland is just a very strange book. She'd wanted to do something Tasmanian as she had a fondness for the place and the people after spending a season working for GraviTas, the prestigious Tasmanian gravy company.

Abandoning that project, she began working on *'The role of the Gin and Tonic in the history of the British Empire'.* It was taking a while and a lot of research was needed. Thankfully she had helpers. A bottle of Gin in her household was an endangered species, even though they weren't concerned about getting malaria. It reminded her of an uncle who always drank whisky in case of snake bites even though he never went anywhere near the bush.

She'd had a brief career writing speeches for a politician and while she wasn't employed for her advice, she found it impossible to resist. Her advice hadn't been popular but she still thought she was right. The politician had framed the issue like this...

"I know we didn't follow through with all that stuff we said last time but this time we really mean it. I know we said that last time, but this time we really, really mean it. You need to trust us."

What do you think?

"Honestly?", asked Liz, not sure she should be put in this position.

Are you prepared to utter a self-curse if it doesn't happen? In ancient times it would be like.... I will complete this task by the last moon of this year or may Zeus, God or the deity of your choice strike me down with a bolt of lightning and smite me from existence. That's the sort of thing the voters want to hear. Not what you said. Show that you've got some skin in the game with your body on the line.

The politician looked her up and down and said, "I don't know about that. Isn't that a bit radical. I mean no one else is taunting God to smite them."

She didn't work there for long.

Her phone "dinged" and snapped her from her reverie. The word-of-the-day had arrived. It was usually a good day if she learnt a new word.

Cacoethes. (noun) Pronounced Ca-co-e-thees. A sudden urge to do something inadvisable.

She wondered why this word hadn't been pointed out to her earlier in life. She'd just used to just call it "fuck it mode".

| 13 |

The night before the business meeting

Monday Evening

The trip had left Ray feeling tired and craving sleep. Productive, but little time for rest. He went into the bathroom and looked at himself in the mirror. His eyes usually stood out as his most captivating feature. A piercing gaze that could cut straight into your soul. Well, that's how they usually looked. At the moment they looked more like two pissholes in the snow surrounded by some craggy cliffs and valleys.

His T-shirt had some colourful food stain down the front. It usually happened when he ate in bed. He looked at the writing on the T-shirt and even in reverse it made him smile. *'News just in from the lead lemming. Everything's fine'.* He took it off, threw it in the bath and rummaged around in his suitcase to pull out another T-shirt. Another favourite. Who was he kidding? They were all favourites. His beloved bespoke T-shirt collection. This one said

'Orwell was an optimist, Darwin was adopted, Schrodinger's being investigated by PETA'.

He'd be starting a series of meetings in less than 8 hours and still had an hour's prep to do. Groggily propping himself up on the couch, he started up his notebook. A quick look at some emails and a few replies left him checking social media notifications.

His mind drifted back to the time while travelling, the cramped plane seats, the hours in the terminals waiting. Why is everything so outrageously expensive? That strange guy Richard, he'd met writing his will. Unsuccessfully trying to snatch some sleep in the toilet and on the plane. His phone buzzed and he glanced down. It was a message that he needed to get in touch with his lawyers. Chance and Norfolk had offices near his home but a phone call would probably be easier. He made a note to call them. Wonder what that's about?

Just then, he had another idea... Pizza anyone can make - Pizza Piss! It's probably already been done, he thought but I should add it to the list anyway. He pulled up his '*Brainstorming ideas'* file and quickly reviewed it for the umpteenth time.

Brainstorming ideas

- Food for drunk people. Breath test the person as they enter the restaurant and then deliver food that's appropriate. If they can't taste it or remember it... it doesn't matter.
- A special day for the Blind.... Nice smells Day. Commercially linked in with fragrance companies and Garden Nurseries.
- An oven in the car that uses the heat of the engine which is largely wasted. You could have a piping hot meal ready as you walk in the door. Same with a picnic. Put a chicken in the car oven, drive to your destination, and it will be absolutely beautiful. Stop all this messing about with BBQs.

- Instead of holding elections, we get all the candidates to play laser tag. It'd be a lot cheaper, more entertaining and would weed out some of the older, slower ones.
- Pre-chewed pencils for the rich.
- An invention that puts Wi-Fi, Bluetooth, power generation and storage in footwear. To be marketed under the name "Clever Clogs".
- A story idea: Two people who think the other one is an arsehole discover through a mutual friend that they're not so different, much to their disgust.
- New choices at the doctors. Choose to receive your flu shot by blow dart or traditional needle. This could really add some excitement to your next visit. Potentially for the doctors at least.
- Clip-on guides for chip shop doorways. If you can't fit through here, you really shouldn't come in. Note: It could appeal to one of those healthy eating organisations.
- Naming rights for natural disasters and their recovery. e.g. This year's Hurricane recovery relief is brought to you by Microsoft, Shell and Nestle.
- Bring back charging money to watch medical procedures. It had been very popular at one time. It was called 'Anatomical Theatre'. Special viewing rooms were built and with modern technology it would be possible to have closeups, video replays and commentary by distinguished former surgeons. Surely there would be a market for that. Subscription services and remote viewing via the internet.
- What is the correct etiquette when you are caught '*turdus interruptus*'. When you are sitting on the toilet, alone in your own home and there is a loud and insistent knocking at the front door? Is the solution, some sort of a handy app on a smartwatch? A smart doorbell system that displays a

message to the caller. To let them know that you are indisposed for some reason and can't come to the door for a few minutes. It could apply to lots of situations like changing a nappy, just getting out of the shower, having sex...

- Shoes, vitamins and bras are poorly designed numbering systems. Surely there's a better way.

He added Pizza Piss to the bottom of the list.

Realising that he wasn't going to get any more work done tonight, he switched on the TV. The volume was too loud and as he tried to focus on the remote control, in the low light to find the volume buttons, he heard ... Coming up, your favourite DIY bloopers show, "Screwed Up!" followed by a completely new series, "Miasmas: Smells that can kill you."

The words sent him down a familiar path. Would TV and movies be as popular if they included smell? The sense of smell is so powerful and some things once smelled can stay with you a lifetime.

Can you imagine watching the news where live smell was transmitted and what a teenager's bedroom could smell like after a solid World of Warcraft session.

It's interesting that we've made our population squeamish.

Supermarkets blur the line around meat products by presenting them on white trays and wrapped in plastic. A generation ago, supermarkets had their own butchery departments. They have mostly gone now. It must have removed a lot of health and safety issues as well as all those butchery smells. Have you noticed how often the deli or meat areas are put close to a bakery, a chicken roasting machine or a coffee vendor.

It seemed to him that a lot of stories are popular because the smell is missing. Any story from ancient history that involves lots of animals and no toilets, for instance.

'Schindler's list' and *'The Shawshank Redemption'* would be quite a different experience if they included the smells. Any action movie where the main person never showers. Subway scenes. Cigarettes and cigars. The list seems to go on and on. He and Liz often noticed how the lack of '*smell-o-vision*' gets used in movies and TV. A character may be hiding while smoking a cigar and none of the other characters notice the smell. They loved spotting those little story problems.

The TV flickered and caught his attention. He picked up the remote and changed channels.

A sober and serious looking BBC journalist type said, "Today a government spokesperson issued the new guidelines for the social distancing of garden gnomes, statues and shop mannequins now that the pandemic appears to be over."

He switched channels again.

There was an interview with the Scottish comedian Frankie Boyle talking about Sick Puppy Syndrome.

Frankie was saying in an almost unintelligible Scottish accent. "The number of people that come up to me and say... you are a sick puppy."

"I don't know why. I don't look like a puppy, do I?" Do I look unwell?

"It doesn't matter whether I am telling a joke about shitting in the street or throwing old ladies off a bridge."

He changed channels again.

It was a fundamental Christian news and weather channel and it was horrifying.

All the bad weather was going to get worse because we had not stoned all our blasphemers and homosexuals or closed down the local seafood restaurant which, incredibly, was still serving shellfish. If something wasn't done about this soon, the droughts would continue and there would obviously be more plagues and pestilence.

Ray was captivated by the speaker. He'd never heard anyone speak like this before. He just didn't think about the fact that there were people alive today who have no problem seeing a connection between people's morality and the weather. No wonder it is so hard to predict.

He'd often thought that it had to be one of the easiest jobs in the world. What other job can you be wrong consistently and somehow that's OK. The only other ones he could think of were economist and politician.

The TV changed volume and drew back his attention as a new ad started.

I don't think I can be bothered with that, he thought and switched off the TV, got undressed, set his alarm and wrestled his way into the bed. How do they get the sheets so tight he wondered? Pushing against the sheets, he tried in vain to turn his feet over. His last thought before sleeping was, I must check out the biceps of the housekeeping staff.

| 14 |

Liz does some research

Wednesday Morning

After putting it off for two days, Liz realised that she had to start. Where to begin?

She gathered all the Adult Services ads for the last month into a single file. Wow, I had no idea there were so many.

She noticed that some names, pictures and businesses were regular but there were quite a few that only advertised once or twice. What does that mean? Is it someone testing the water? Just trying it to see if they like it? Only doing it to pay a bill?

Liz had no idea. She also realised that she was going to have to make contact with some of these people and that was revealing things about her too. She was feeling highly embarrassed. I'll do a bit more research, she thought safely, and that'll put it off a bit longer.

Over the next couple of days, she collected, collated and mapped all the ads from the last year. This painted a slightly different picture. There were far more different people offering services than she'd expected.

During the research, she'd also found that her own ideas about this whole area were based on some things she'd been told growing up and never challenged. She was judging everyone involved and that's not the role of a journalist. Okay, as my editor said, I am a journalist. I have the framed thing on the wall to prove it. Treat this the same as any other story. Who, What, Where, When, Why and How. The usual starting places. It's a bit different to politics where the questions are usually whose fault? who pays? and who wins and loses etc?

For this assignment, some better questions could be...

1. Who are the characters involved?
2. Where are the settings and locations?
3. How does the economics of it all work?
4. What are the top 10 most common questions that the person on the street doesn't know but would like to?

She leaned back in her chair. Okay, now I am starting to get somewhere.

Flicking slowly through the paper versions of some of the ads, Liz then used her computer to turn the whole folder's worth of images into a collage. As she looked between the two, she noticed that overall, the bulk of the ads were text. It wasn't pornish. Not lots of blatant sex on display. The pictures were mostly of faces, not whole bodies.

What does that mean?

She put all the text into a word cloud generator and tried a couple of variations until she noticed a few words stick out. Okay, this is going in a different direction than I imagined. She did some YouTube searches and found a video by Nicole Emma called '*What a sex worker can teach us about human connection.*'

According to the video, it's not just about sex and lots of weird stuff. It's also about things like intimacy, connection, touch and appealing to a lot of lonely and heartbroken people.

Who'd've thought?

| 15 |

Ray's story

The Past

Ray's mother always told him that he was as beautiful as he was clever. Until his marriage, he'd taken that as a compliment. Now he wasn't so sure. A seed of doubt had been placed.

Growing up, his next-door neighbours were the Barlow family. There were 2 older girls and one boy his age called Seth. Seth was one of those kids who could really live up or down to his name. His nickname at school was "Set the".

It was clear that Seth Barlow was heading down one of two paths... Socio or Psycho. No one was really sure. There was a fair bit of speculation but mostly expressions of gratitude that he wasn't their kid or family member.

While the families lived next door to each other, Ray and Seth played and interacted just by being the same age and living in close proximity. They got along fine, just the two of them but they lost touch after the Barlows moved to another city.

Ray's life had changed dramatically after that when a large, middle aged am-dram singer moved into the Barlow family's old place. He'd heard the expression, *'It's not over til the fat lady sings'* and here she was singing on a regular basis just near his bedroom window.

Was this the beginning of the end? Should he start getting his affairs in order? He considered. He didn't really have any affairs; he was only 9 going on 10.

Is this fate? What had he done to deserve this? Is there anything he can do to prevent it? He'd worked himself into a right old state that year. All completely silently and entirely in his head.

As a musician, the fat lady's ability was inversely proportional to her enthusiasm, which is the bit that always upsets people.

He liked music. Growing up, there was lots of music in his household as his mother liked listening to exercise tapes. She never actually did the exercises but she got *something* out of it. She liked having them going in the background and knew it was a bit odd but lots of people love watching cooking shows and never cook. It must be part of that human fascination we have with watching other people work.

His mother's father, his Granddad, had lived with them for a few years until he died and he'd sit for much of the day in his favourite chair and watch TV. Sometimes certain people only had to appear on the TV for his mum to be reaching for the 'Spit and Bile Remover' (Pat. Pending).

Over the years his mother came to recognise that certain people caused the spit and bile to achieve near Olympian distances, perhaps only rivalled by the long, high and triple jumpers combined. That is, further than you would expect by a long way and higher up the room than you would've thought possible.

Around news time, she would put on her specially made holster containing the Spit and Bile Remover (Pat. Pending) on one side and a selection of three cloths on the other.

Scott Morrison or Rupert Murdoch appearing on the TV had her drawing like a gunslinger.

Whatever the topic he would say, "That's appalling and someone should do something about it!" It seemed to get right up his nose as he'd currently delegated the government and they didn't seem to be doing very well.

His mother had told and retold the story to anyone that would listen for many years.

She'd been walking past a spruiker outside a small shop. The spruiker had the shitty microphone, shitty amplifier and that *'style'* of delivery that is universally recognised as... this person will do and say absolutely anything to sell something to me.

She'd made the mistake of making eye contact, which launched him into his spiel.

"Do you have a partner, spouse or friend with strong views? Do you have people around you who are upset and frustrated about politics or life in general... and they want to tell you about it."

Without waiting for a response, he continued enthusiastically, "I have what you need. Spit and Bile Remover" (Pat. Pending).

"It easily removes their spit, bile and dribble from furniture, screens and tablets. It also works on pets and children. Just double the dose to remove general bile residue."

"Now", he said looking her straight in the eye, "how many would you like?"

While her father was alive, she'd bought lots. He was a complete bugger really and didn't mind winding his daughter up. She was a big fan of the Queen and insisted on watching the Queen's annual address every year. He'd always refer to it as, *'The Regina Monologues'* just to annoy her.

In his family's tradition, the first born child is experimented upon as the parents try out all their ideas on how to fix what was done to them in their own childhoods. As you'd expect, this leads to mixed and unpredictable results. The approach applied to the second child, the second attempt, is usually better, but sometimes the parents are determined to persevere with their ideas. The third child usually gets a fairly easy run if the parents are still tied up with whatever they are trying to do to the first two children. He was number five of six, which is nearly a Borg name. By the time he came along, they'd long ago given up on those high ideals after they realised how physically exhausting it is.

As the youngest of three brothers, he was able to see how his mother controlled his older brothers and sisters as they got bigger. As the situation changed and she couldn't just pick them up or hold them down, her approach changed to a self-binding psychological leash. An age-old approach that has worked for so many mothers and religions around the world for such a long time.

He'd played in a few bands in his younger days, starting with *'The Scoobie Doobie Brothers'* and then *'Crash and Burn'.* The best known locally would have been the duo *'Whelmed and Gruntled'.* When another player joined them briefly, they oscillated between *'The Good, the Bad and the Fugly'* and *'Girth, Wind and Fire'.*

They were playing originals but the punters wanted to hear covers. Their final gig had been like the old joke. The band called out, what do you want us to play?

"Dominos, eight ball or cards", yelled back the crowd.

He'd known a lot of musicians over those years and like many from that era he'd devoted his early years to wine, women and song, not that he sang a lot. Many of his bandmates spent a lot of their twenties researching drunken nymphomaniacs... I s'pose everybody needs a hobby.

Since then, the march of time had proved relentless and much to his dismay, a lot of his favourite music from when he was growing up was now being used in city centres to keep teenagers out.

Another reluctant discovery in his early twenties was that while some people can wear all white clothes and drink red wine or cook with turmeric, he wasn't one of them. Every time he tried, he either heavily stained and ruined his clothes, a work bench or the utensils or someone else's clothes, workbench or utensils.

His idea of fun as a teenager was to put random things in people's pockets, bags or supermarket trolleys. He rarely got to see the punchline but his imagination did a great job of filling in the blanks anyway. He could picture the look on their faces when they put their hand in their pocket and found an unfamiliar shape, like one Lego brick. They would find the unfamiliar shape and stop in their tracks; the brow would furrow and they'd bring the object out and stare at it intently like it was an alien artefact or oopart. Distributing a 1000-piece jigsaw could last a whole summer.

He kept an eye out for women with very large handbags. As far as he could see, they could fit a lot in these and they may not actually empty it or get to the bottom of it for weeks, months or years. Same reaction. The puzzled look. The detailed examination. The rumination. The WTF look. The best bit was when someone puts it back in their pocket or handbag just in case it is important to someone in their life.

He figured some people were still carting around random crap that he'd put in their handbags years ago. It still made him smile and therefore had no intention of stopping. This was going really well until he found a piece of random crap in his own pocket. Uh-Oh. Someone else is doing it. Touché.

He'd always been fascinated by detective fiction and had worked through the local libraries collection. In his youth he liked the stories of Arthur Conan Doyle, Agatha Christie, Raymond Chandler, G. K. Chesterton, E. W. Hornung and anything with a mystery and a twist he could get his hands on. He'd even considered taking it up as a career and looked into going to a detective school but it was expensive and time consuming, so he just pretended to be famous detectives in the private universe of his mind instead. Mostly Sherlock Holmes or Poirot but sometimes a bit Father Brown even though he didn't know a lot about being Catholic.

As it happened, this was one of the things that he and Liz shared. She did it too. This combined with the love of science fiction and comedy was a large part of the glue that held them together.

One of his early girlfriends who was probably an undiagnosed schizophrenic and regularly rode the bi-polar express was mostly good people... well... except one. He always counted it as a threesome if anybody asked, which they rarely did. He'd mentioned it to a friend once, who'd told him very definitely "No". Sleeping with a bi-polar person or being held down for your colonoscopy doesn't count as a threesome.

People riding the bi-polar express made him think about the similarities to his sister-in-law. She'd been in hospital recently after having an accident in her car. It was so strange to hear the family describe her as *'stable'*. From his experience, if they were trying to describe that she was nearly back to normal, they should have said she's a self-absorbed drama queen who really gets a lot of value out of schadenfreude... but that's not the medical professional way.

He'd dabbled a bit with sport in his teens but playing music and partying began taking up most of his weekends and so he drifted away. He'd played soccer, cricket and tennis and apart from being in some teams that had nearly won some things, it wasn't his natural calling.

Cricket was probably his worst one and as a cricketer, he had failed but with magnificent style. As he watched the bowler run in, he was reading all the body language, facial expressions and every indicator to pick which shot he was going to commit to. As the bowler released the ball, he moved into a perfectly formed off drive stroke. Unfortunately, he missed the ball completely and stood in perfect form, looking back at the missing bails.

Well... that was how he remembered it. It probably wouldn't stand up in court but he wasn't remembering under oath. His opinion was that self-delusion is a private matter and is essential to all humans. It should be considered a basic human right. How could any of us survive without a bit of active self-delusion? He'd always considered it one of his superpowers. Self-delusion as an art form. He'd talked many times to the family doctor over the years about these sorts of things.

The doctor had once told his father that he was suffering from '*TMB*' and his father had felt reassured by this. It was good to be able to label his symptoms until he googled it. *'Too Many Birthdays'*. When the doctor delivered his diagnosis on his father's failing health, he told him that while he was a man of many parts, unfortunately not enough of them were willing to continue working together to keep him going. It'd softened the blow slightly.

Ray often thought of him as Dr Strange.

At one point in his early twenties, Dr Strange told him that he was suffering from '*Descartes Disease*' and that he should look it up when he got home and probably get it made into a T-Shirt or wallpaper for his desktop. He was beginning to realise that this Doctor had a very unusual sense of humour... if that's what this was. After a bit of googling, he realised he meant that he was doubting. Doubting everything and to a level that was paralysing him.

At some level he understood that the doctor was right to some degree but it didn't take away the fact that it was right to doubt these things. Isn't that part of critical thinking, detective work and that sort of thing? Some even saw it as the basis for the modern scientific method. The more he thought about it, the more it was hard to deny that when you doubt everything, you find that one day the world can drop out from underneath you and there is no solid ground to grab on to or rely upon.

Sometimes he'd managed to really scare himself. He wondered if he could accidentally think himself out of existence. Were there some thoughts that a person just should never, ever think? He'd read of people suffering from this when they try to control their heart beating or heart rate. The belief that you are consciously controlling your heart is very powerful. The horror thought is '*how do you return control to automatic?*' A similar thing is reported when people try to learn to hold their breath for long periods.

This seemed like dangerous ground.

| 16 |

In the foyer

Wednesday Morning

Ray was early and they were late. He'd been waiting in the foyer for over an hour and checked his presentation, his emails, his social media and the contents of his wallet. After completing all this he sat staring around the foyer looking for anything to keep him awake and alert.

Draped across the foyer wall was a large advertisement declaring a conference of some description. Whatever it was, it seemed clear that he needed to act quickly. As he focused on the whole splendour and grandness of it all, he was captured by the slogan *'The more you fail, the more you grow. All the lessons that failure has taught us, makes success inevitable.'*

He pondered it briefly. He'd certainly had his fair share of failures. Is that how it works? You have so many failures until it's your turn? Like being in the Public Service? What had he learnt from his failures? Did he have time to consider all this? Drawing an involuntarily dejected breath, he realised that he did. He thought back over his recent business ideas.

He'd been trying to get interest in his novelty condom branding, the *"I kid you not'* condom. No success so far.

A movement across the foyer made him focus on a well-dressed couple who were engaged in a highly animated but whispered conversation. He couldn't hear any of it but he tried to work out what they were saying. His amateur detective genes and imagination kicked in as they became spies and supervillains. The animation must be because their master plan was unravelling or they were about to be caught and trying to work out how to escape.

He was delightfully lost in these daydreams when he heard his name being called. This shattered the internal imaginings and unceremoniously returned him to the external world.

"That's me", Ray stammered as he started to rise from his chair.

After being seated for over an hour, both his feet had gone to sleep and he found he couldn't get out of the chair. He started to lift his body with his arms but his legs just didn't want to hold any weight. Oh brilliant! What am I going to do now, he thought?

"Sorry, I seem to be having a bit of trouble."

"Do you need medical help?", asked the receptionist using her caring professional tone.

"I think it will come right soon; my feet have just gone to sleep."

The receptionist and a passerby helped him out of his seat where he stood uncertainly, balanced between their shoulders as the blood started to return to his lower extremities.

"Thank you very much. Both of you. They must have gone to sleep. Sorry, I didn't mean the wait wasn't worth it. What am I saying? Now where do I go?"

The receptionist pointed with a look at the only door in the room apart from the entrance.

"Of course, sorry, what am I saying? I've only been staring at it for the last hour. You must think I'm a complete twat. This is so important to me, you know, I just don't want to mess it up."

The passerby asked him if he was okay to stand on his own or wanted a glass of water? He said "Yes" to the first and "No" to the second. The passerby then let him go and walked through the only door.

He turned to the receptionist. "Is that who I'm going to see?"

She suddenly looked like Garfield the cat at his most condescending. "Yes"

Oh shit. Talk about how to make a good first impression.

| 17 |

The next Friday phone call

Friday Evening

Liz's mother was in complaining mode.

"Do you remember when your sister went to hospital after her accident with a concussion and we said it was the only time in her life where she was ever described as stable."

"Yes, I remember", Liz said cautiously.

"I love her. She's my eldest daughter but, you know, she's the sort of person when you're going to hell in a handbasket, wants to not only be in control of the basket, but all the way down keeps telling you that control of the basket is more important than the destination."

"Yes. A game played by politicians around the world throughout time. The politics and practices of the schoolyard", said Liz, with a touch of cynicism.

"Be nice. She's still your sister", said her mother obliviously unaware of the double standards and hypocrisy at play.

Her mother distributed any information she had freely and widely with no regard for anything as trivial as people's feelings.

She considered it community service. A well-informed community was better off, she said repeatedly. Not everyone around her saw it in the same way. There was much speculation in the family that the witticism "gossip is the only thing that travels faster than light" was based on someone who knew her.

Gossip is such a strange beast. Communities rely on the interchange of information but when you live in the one community all your life, you get to know all sorts of things about the people around you. Her mother, aunts and sister were the type of people that anytime a person is mentioned they always made sure to drop in the most gut-wrenching story about them. To Liz this was called "playing the man", which was a sports term, most likely from soccer and short for the full expression "playing the man, not the ball". There was a wilful spite involved and an intention to bring every person down a peg or two.

They also tended to do the same with first time pregnancies and drag out every horrifying story they knew, in order to make sure that the newly expectant mum was properly prepared. It usually just terrified the shit out of them and made their eyes grow larger and larger until they were the size of saucers. When they reached that size, they felt her work was done and that they'd successfully conveyed all the risks.

A sweet older teacher at high school, who knew her mother and her aunts, had once told Liz that a good way to measure yourself was based on the expression, "If you haven't got something nice to say about someone or something, don't say anything". As Liz tried to work with this idea, she found that she could go very long periods without uttering a sound. Eventually, she got better at it, but her mother was always a challenge.

Anyway, her mother continued, "your niece Zoe is staying with me for a few weeks while she does a unit for her course."

"What's she studying?"

"Engineering. She's been telling me about reversibility and irreversibility", not mentioning that she was glancing at the chapter heading of the open textbook on the table.

"Wasn't that by one of the Bronte sisters?", Liz joked.

"Are you still thinking you're going to be a standup comedian?", her mother continued pouring water on her ambitions again.

"It's been nice to catch up with her. That reminds me, she's been telling me about her summer job as an assistant to some nutty professor who was trying to convince Meerkats that everything is OK. There is no need to stand up like that. I think she said he was Darwinian but I'm not sure."

"What was he researching?"

"Not sure but she said that early on in his career he got a lot of funding to try to find out whether the Neanderthals were able to achieve a good work/life balance?"

"Sounds a bit like a guy I have been writing about. Was it George King?"

"I don't know dear. What did he do?"

"Early in his career he pioneered research into whether there is a relationship between which side of the bed you sleep on and your politics."

"Is that true?" Her mother was intrigued, then realised, "That was a joke, wasn't it?"

"Yes Ma. You got me. Do you have plans for the weekend?"

"Not really. Just the market on Saturday morning, bowls in the afternoon and then off to see a local play. Sunday, I'll probably just go to church and the jazz club in the afternoon."

"Right. Just normal then", said Liz amazed at how active her mum still was at 72.

"What about you dear?"

"Just the usual, work around the house and garden on Saturday and then my usual Sunday morning. Tai Chi followed by Chai Tea.", Liz smiled repeating one of her favourite lines.

"Hmmm. OK, comedian, let me have it. What have you got this week?"

"Thanks Ma,"

"Two people sitting reading the paper. One turns to the other. Now that's a headline you rarely see. "Swimwear model wins Nobel prize". What should the punch line be?"

"I really don't know", said her mother after a long pause.

Okay what about... "I heard on the news tonight that an acupuncturist was stabbed multiple times with his own instruments during a break-in. Apparently, he has never felt better."

"Very good dear, but I still don't think you should give up your day job just yet. By the way, your brother is coming over this Wednesday and it would be good for us all to get together. We haven't all been together since Christmas. If you can't make it, we can Zoom. I know how to do it now."

Her brother won a scholarship through the Lions Club which allowed him to attend university in England and after four years emerged with a degree of smugness. He was now a pot smoking minor celebrity pastry and dessert chef. Family gatherings were always a bit awkward as Ray didn't really like or trust him. The problem was that he was too skinny. To Ray's way of thinking, it made him a bit like a drug dealer who doesn't partake in his own concoctions. He supplies the sugar, salt and fat in enticing packages but takes no responsibility for all the obese people and their medical problems. If he did it outside schools or to children, you would think he would be identified and put on a register... not given his own TV show.

Liz mentally reviewed any good, legitimate reasons why she might have to travel or be away for that night.

No good reasons sprang to mind… Nothing.

Bugger.

"Sure Ma, Ray will be away but I'll be here. Call me when you're ready."

| 18 |

Angie's insurance

Three years ago

Angie studied the document intently. It was a list of her clients, their contact details and the dates and times of their appointments. This was her insurance. She only had this small group of regular clients and they paid her handsomely. Apart from being blackmailed into it in the first place, the money made it a workable arrangement.

When she'd graduated and became Angela Murray, Bachelor of Laws, she'd stopped working at the club and began looking for work seriously. She applied to all the top firms through their graduate recruitment programs and was starting to receive some offers.

She was surprised and alarmed to be offered a fast track to partner if she agreed to a regular session with one of the senior partners of the firm. He recognised her from the club and was prepared to bend a few rules to make it happen. It was a strange situation for her as he was a very handsome and influential man in his late 40s. She would normally have considered him out of her league.

After a few nights of soul-searching, she agreed as long as she could put some protections in place for herself.

Firstly, create the document that she was now holding. It would automatically be sent to a select group of power brokers that could make things happen if for any reason everything in her life went pear shaped, like in the event of her death or serious accident. She wanted those protections. The extensive resources and support of a senior law firm partner enabled her to design the document and the process.

If anything happened to her, Cassie would get looked after and if it was suspicious in any way her death or accident would be investigated properly and justice done.

He set up a generous retainer to allow him one 'visit' per month and this side income dwarfed her starting salary at the law firm. They would meet on the first Tuesday of every month in a luxury hotel suite. She would be paid a monthly retainer with the first month in advance. He also encouraged her to make the same arrangement with three other people and provided her with a list of people to choose from. All wealthy. All keen on privacy and discretion. One session per month each. The legal partner was week one, a judge was week two, a businessman in week three and a media bigwig in week four. They each got three hours per month and in one year she'd be able to buy her apartment. It was a hard offer to refuse.

| 19 |

Back home

Saturday Morning

Liz got up early and started to make some breakfast. She got sidetracked looking for the pup and only came back to the kitchen to turn off the smoke alarm and throw out her first attempt. After opening every window and door, the smoke quickly dissipated like a promise in a politician's head.

It was Saturday morning and the smell of burnt toast lingered as they were having breakfast. Ray looked up from reading the news on his tablet and asked, "Who was the first person that helped you through the *'It's not fair'* internal dialogue?"

"I don't know that anyone ever really did", Liz replied, "I just learned not to think about it. I manage the feelings that arise when I dwell on things, because if I don't manage them, it rarely turns out well... and I can generate some feelings on demand if I want. They are part of my toolkit for changing my state.

What about you and why do you ask?"

My grandmother. She always knew something was up without me telling her. I s'pose she'd dealt with teenagers before. I was just reading about refugees. A lot of them have a really rough time, just because of where they were born. It doesn't seem fair.

He wandered off to his home office and tried to do some work but found it hard to settle. As he looked around his office, he could see some framed certificates and a couple of trophies he'd received. The trophies were both jokes. '*Most Improved Runner-up*'. That'd been funny at the time. The other one was for '*Best Shot of the Series*' from his tennis club for an incredibly lucky and unintentional shot when he somehow put the correct spin on the ball to make it go over the net and then instantly recoil back again to his own side, making it completely impossible to hit. He still had no idea how he did it. They'd all had a good laugh about it at the awards night.

Beside the trophies were copies of the one book he'd written. It was 15 years ago now when they both fancied themselves as writers. His one book had been a surprising hit. '*The Art and Optimism of Cord Wiggling*'. He certainly had been surprised for one. It still provided a surprisingly good royalty stream. He would like to write more but hadn't been able to think up a snappy and catchy title that was as good as the first one. He'd considered reworking the old classic '*Footprints in the sand*' into '*Carbon footprints in the sand*'... but couldn't get past the title.

He looked at the clock on the computer. 9:30 am. He had a few hours before he had to take Liz to the airport to pick up her friend. He'd no idea what to expect really. All he knew was that they were about the same age and had been pen pals since primary school. The Great Dane grew up in a remote town called Skagen, pronounced Skay-gn, right at the top tip of Denmark. He'd looked it up on Google Maps. It was as far north as you could go and still be in Denmark. It looked like a small fishing village with very colourful yellow houses. Apparently since the 1870's it was a popular place for writers and artists. The Great Dane, whose real name was Sofia Hansen, now lived in Copenhagen and did something medical at the University of Copenhagen.

Liz had also done some research and found that heavy drinking was pretty standard in Denmark, in fact, about half the population regularly drinks to get drunk. There was also a custom of planning a quiet day following a heavy session to deal with the expected hangover.

She said to Ray, "I think we should plan for a heavy night and make no plans for tomorrow. There is a fair chance that she'll be able to drink us both under the table. According to Google the most popular drinks apart from beers are whisky, gin, vodka and a cherry liqueur. I've already got bottles of gin as usual and a bottle of Laphroaig whisky. There's a carton of beer. Carlsberg is popular there but I thought it would be better to have something from here. I picked up a carton of your usual 6.66% Moo Brew IPA and a carton of Crown Lager."

Keeping up a form of communication with someone for thirty-odd years but rarely actually meeting in person seemed a bit odd to Ray. They'd exchanged Christmas cards each year after their initial letter writing as primary school children and met once in their late teens when Sofia stayed with Liz's family for a week over the summer holidays. He imagined it was just one of those things that get encouraged when you live in remote villages. Find a school in another remote part of the world and get the kids to write to each other.

Ray and Liz found they could only name a few facts about Denmark. Hans Christian Anderson, Copenhagen, Lego, Princess Mary, Sandy Toksvig, Hamlet was a Prince of Denmark and something being rotten in the state of Denmark. Was it fish? Was this before Denmark was a country? It wasn't an impressive list. Ray thought Denmark had something to do with Greenland, although he couldn't remember what.

Liz's mother was a big fan of Sandi Toksvig and that program where she, Stephen Fry and assorted guests torture and psychologically mess with Alan Davies. How they have trained him to say '*Blue whale*' would impress Pavlov. Ray was pretty sure that John Lloyd deserved at least some of the blame.

He pottered around for the rest of the morning and then made a light lunch as they discussed what they planned to do with their visitor. It sounded like pick her up, get her settled and then start drinking and talking. Nothing complicated. She'd not asked to be taken anywhere, she was just curious to meet Liz in person again and spend some time together.

As they started to get ready Ray had a '*Hamlet*' moment. It often happened when he was about to go on a long car journey. To pee or not to pee, that was the question. To him, it was nobler in the mind not to suffer any slings, arrows or full bladders. He lightened his load.

The drive to the airport was uneventful and he dropped Liz at the terminal and went in search of a parking space. He was still driving around looking for somewhere to stop temporarily when he got the phone call to come back to the terminal and pick them up.

He'd made sure that he had no preconceived idea of what she'd look like after the dog thing and she wasn't any of those.

She looked like a lot of women he'd seen in magazines... usually under the heading '*Before*'. The other distinguishing feature was that she liked to talk. A lot.

As they drove from the airport the Great Dane reeled off a seemingly endless list of Superman's or Kal-El's lesser-known cousins. As they were going past a fabric shop that sold linen products she talked about Flan-El and Past-El. The renewable energy farm was run by his cousin Solarpan-El. Another cousin who sold camping equipment was called Clark Tent. Ray hadn't heard any of these before and thought he might enjoy a mind like this for a weekend.

It seemed that she was very involved in her work in the medical industry and many of her stories were work related. Just before they reached home, she told a story about a forensic expert she worked with who specialised in Dactyloscopy and produced world class facial composites. He was eventually promoted and was reported in the staff magazine as being *'The artist formerly known as Prints'*. At this point Ray started to wonder if she was pulling his leg. (She was.)

She described herself as a mischief maker who was always looking for a way to get some fun into her day. Like when she'd once asked at a very serious symposium, what the panel thought about renaming the duodenum as we have now moved to the metric system. She riffed on that for a while. Shylock demanding .45359 kilograms of flesh, a dollar for your thoughts after adjusting for inflation, walking 1.60934 kilometres in someone else's shoes or changing the TV show *'Six feet under'* in metric countries to *'1.8288 metres under'*.

They arrived home, moved her suitcases into the spare room, settled around the kitchen table and opened beers. The Great Dane continued to tell stories and generally be entertaining.

Apparently, she'd conducted early research to calculate how many carbs equals 1 hug. This had set her up as someone that big pharma could do business with. It was a shame that she was too young for the "no causal link between tobacco and cancer" years as she could have contributed to that campaign in positive ways that would have confused and confounded nearly everyone for at least another decade.

As they moved onto the G & T's, Sofia Hansen found her soapbox and moved onto her favourite topic. She began in a voice that was more appropriate in an auditorium than in the kitchen. "The challenge for this generation is selling the idea that the health industry is about health". It is an easy mistake to make but as Sir Humphrey pointed out, "You get rid of the difficult bits in the title". She seemed to like to quote from *'Yes Minister'* a lot.

The Great Dane had found her stride. "Imagine for a moment", she said, "the three basic approaches to health and medicine. What would be the outcome if they were properly funded and implemented?"

"Firstly, consider health as a private matter and it's an individual's responsibility to manage, procure and contract services with doctors and other medical professionals. The role of hospitals is effectively Accident and Emergency. People with ongoing conditions make arrangements with private hospices and clinics. The effect of community health on the community isn't calculated or talked about."

"Or secondly, health is a mixture of private and public responsibility. There is an onus placed on citizens to look after their own health. To not be obese, don't smoke too much, don't drink too much, take exercise, eat good food, find ways to manage your stresses that don't include too much smoke, drink, pills or other forms of *'fuck it'* behaviour."

"The third way is something like a military or Star Trek version where your body and its good function is a responsibility of the state. The state monitors your health continuously through simple devices like smart watches. This continuous monitoring allows for very quick responses to situations through personalised feedback."

This was all a bit too serious for Liz and Ray and they eventually managed to move her off this topic and back on to funnier medical stories. She seemed to have lots of them which made her good company and the evening went by quickly.

Ray remembered some he was sure he'd use down the pub tomorrow. He enjoyed her stories about getting into trouble for using household renovation terms for plastic surgery procedures. Terms like "spakfilla" and "cut and shut". The problem for her more formal colleagues was, they worked. Non-medical people understand these terms. In her mind it was better communication.

As the night went on they moved through beers to G & T's to whisky. Around midnight, Ray went off to bed, leaving them alone to catch up. The conversation had turned to romantic relationships and sex. The Great Dane had just finished saying that while she enjoyed sex, it'd all gotten a bit complicated lately and how her life was much better and simpler now that her choice of lover was dishwasher safe.

That had seemed like a perfect time for Ray to say goodnight.

| 20 |

In the pub

Sunday Afternoon

Ray arrived at the pub late, nursing a hangover and started looking around for his mate. He was usually easy to spot. His friend Gabe was so tall that at large events he usually became the rendezvous point. It worked nearly everywhere except for when they went to the basketball.

He saw him by the window talking to another regular. He couldn't remember his name but he had the sort of face and beard that made you unsure if he was a short, bearded man standing upright or a tall naked man touching his toes.

It's a shock to most people at first and thankfully he didn't flinch like he used to. The hairs in his nose looked like he'd snorted a meerkat or some small hairy creature.

As Ray approached, he caught the tail end of their conversation.

Meerkat man was saying, "I thought they were calling me "Yakult" but it turns out I'd misheard them".

Aah, there you are Ray. Do you want a drink?

"I don't mind if I do", jumped in Meerkat Man.

"What's new in your life?", his tall mate asked when they were finally alone.

"Not much, still trying to get someone interested in one of my projects", Ray replied, "What about you?"

"Mollys got a new project. She's trying to raise money to set up a helpline for people who don't or won't follow advice or listen. She says we can do it fairly cheaply and these people desperately need our support. At least I think that's what she said. Although now I say it out loud, it doesn't actually make sense. Perhaps I've got that wrong." He smiled a mischievous smile.

They chatted over a few beers until Ray excused himself and headed for the toilets. When he got there, the urinal was full, so he headed into the only remaining stall. Once there he decided that he may as well use its full functionality or *'Drop the kids off at the pool'*, as Liz used to so eloquently put it.

It wasn't an overly sophisticated pub or clientele which he mostly liked and while he sat and waited for his biology to complete its processes, he heard a typical pub conversation between two twits.

Twit One was saying, "She keeps saying that I don't listen to her. At least I think that's what she said. I told her, I think you have the marriage vows and the Amazon returns policy mixed up. So I need a place to stay for tonight if that's OK", he said confidently. "It's just for tonight", he said, not quite as confidently.

"I see. That could be a problem", said Twit Two.

"What you mean?" asked Twit One.

"My missus has been trying to get in shape."

"Yeh..."

She told me about it and I said, "What shape are you going for this time?"

"So, I was hoping to stay at your place tonight. Who would have thought that we'd both be in the doghouse at the same time."

Ray put his ear buds in and continued listening to an episode of "The Unbelievable Truth". Anything to block out those idiots.

As he returned to the bar, he heard the band start up. The sound reminded him of someone starting an untuned Harley while desexing a reluctant and unsedated cat. It didn't agree with him. This was sounding like one of those bands that he'd enjoy better from a distance. The greater the distance the greater the enjoyment.

He was pleased Liz hadn't come along today, as she would have been annoyed. She preferred music that was more tuneful and melodic with great rhythms. Typical drummer.

She'd once told him that "Music is a way to deliberately disturb a person's equilibrium and then take credit for returning it... if you do it well, the surprising part is that people like that and will pay handsomely for it."

Later that night when his bladder was full again, he went back to the toilet in search of skid marks, detritus and other entrenched toilet stains to attack. He knew the satisfaction that came from this simple pleasure that helped clean up the mess of others.

He looked around. The whole bathroom was meticulously clean. Damn, he thought. I was looking forward to that part.

He found himself patiently waiting for the liquid that was no longer required to be expelled from his body. Experience told him that there was absolutely nothing he could do that would speed up the process. He'd tried before. Squeezing this or pushing that, it only got you so far... and then you just had to wait. He resigned himself to it. Thank God he wasn't a whistler, because this was the perfect time.

The stream went on so long that he started to notice how patient he was being. Then he noticed how pleased he was with being this patient... Aaah... another benefit of alcohol.

He wasn't taxing his body in any way. He was just waiting for it to do its thing and then he could get back to putting in more liquid, in the same inefficient way, then come back here and repeat the process sometime in the future.

This was really taking some time now. He was starting to go philosophical and ask some of the why questions.

Why was it taking so long? Why was it really necessary to put all this liquid in to get the effect? Weren't there drugs that do that? Should he take up drugs instead? Drug users don't seem to have this issue, although they do seem to have a few other problems. They are more '*head in the toilet*' problems rather than '*standing over it for long periods of time problems*'. Although enough alcohol can have you inspecting the inside of a random toilet bowl with a more intense scrutiny and affection than you would have imagined possible. He could vaguely remember, many an hour in his band days, when a toilet bowl had temporarily been his best friend.

Someone had once shown him the description of '*Dexedrine*' from Wikipedia which is an ADHD medication. It said it's also used as '*an athletic performance and cognitive enhancer, and recreationally as an aphrodisiac and euphoriant*'. People wonder why some are drawn to drugs. Doesn't that describe what most people want?

He eventually returned to Gabe who'd been joined by another local who was being asked by his tall friend, "Is your missus still on her diet?"

"She started off great. I mean, she was going really well until one day recently, she ate her diet book...she put it in the blender, mashed it into a pulp and then fried it in lots of butter and garlic. I asked her what happened but she didn't want to talk about it... in a most emphatic manner. If that'd been the other way around, do you think I would've ever heard the end of it."

"Just another one of those double standards mate. Is she going to go back on it?" Gabe asked, showing genuine concern.

"I haven't had the heart to ask the question yet. I thought I'd just wait a few months and see if she brings it up naturally. It's a dilemma. I was sort of hoping that she'll eventually realise that this is a completely self-imposed pressure to look like a different person at her cousin's wedding at the end of the year."

"I know that if I don't point that out sometime soon, then somehow it'll become my fault that she can't fit into whatever ridiculous thing she used to wear decades ago and thinks she should be able to again." The local thought about this for a moment and glazed over at the imagery.

Gabe said, "Look, if she is really miserable leading up to the wedding, she'll share that misery with you on a daily basis. So, in the interests of general peace and harmony, is it worth making a little fuss now instead of having months of drama in the lead up to the wedding."

"Probably. What should I do?"

"Well, like it or not", Gabe explained, "you have to encourage and support her in the diet now. Start again and keep starting again if she falls off the wagon. Keep reminding her how you'll both feel at that wedding. She'll look and feel fantastic and you'll have supported and encouraged her all the way."

He looked doubtful.

"That sounds all great in theory Gabe but let me get this straight. What you are saying is, that if I go through a certain amount of hell daily for the rest of the year keeping her on the wagon, my life will be better for a few days around the wedding and I just have to encourage and support my wife in her health, diet and exercise choices from now until the wedding."

He looked to Gabe for confirmation. Gabe was nodding supportively.

"I know that sounds really sensible, but I don't think I can put up with all that whinging and moaning on a daily basis for months and months. I'd rather deal with the whinging and moaning over a much shorter time."

Gabe said, "That's up to you mate" and wandered over to Ray, washing his hands of the whole affair.

| 21 |

The meeting

Monday Morning

The dreaded day arrived. The editor's monthly meeting on long term projects.

Liz looked around the room. A whole bunch of other nervous people, sipping coffees and engaging in small talk waiting for the tsunami to arrive.

A TV was on in the corner showing some *'talking heads'* on the news channel.

Liz nervously flicked through her notes.

Nothing had changed. Same as a few minutes ago. What a surprise.

And then they were off! The editor arrived moving fast in some colourful flowing and tight clothing combination that was a bit weird but was probably high fashion and expensive.

"Okay. Let's get started", the editor declared, naturally assuming that everyone was listening.

"Turn that thing down will you", waving at some random person without looking up.

There was a brief silence while we waited for someone to pick up the remote.

In that brief moment, the news reporter said... "the prime minister, a well-known count- ".

It was an unfortunate time to cut a word short and the silence extended even longer as everyone in the room digested and processed what had just happened. Did he just say what I think he said? Eyes darted around the room as everyone silently questioned each other. "Did you hear that too?"

"Obviously it was cut off", said the editor, "He was in the middle of saying country or something similar. Now let's get down to business."

"Where are all your projects up to? Let's start on my left."

"Liz, I have arranged for you to interview that advocate for a sex workers alliance. She's an eloquent speaker and is very passionate about the subject. After talking with her I'm sure you'll have lots of material and different viewpoints to consider."

"Sue will send you the details. I suggest you allow a bit of time for this as she has a lot to say. Consider her your guide to this other world. I have to admit that after talking with her, I'm wondering whether this particular article shouldn't go way beyond its original scope."

"That reminds me everyone, remember our celebration this Friday night. 7pm at my place. Don't be late. I expect to see you all there with bells on."

Liz heard someone on her right whisper, "Not literally... surely?"

| 22 |

The work party

Friday Night

Ray accompanied Liz to her work party. They were celebrating winning some award that he'd never heard of and the editor was hosting a small party for her staff at her own place.

As the guests were awkwardly mingling around waiting for the beneficial effects of the alcohol to kick in, Ray went to the kitchen to get fresh drinks when he unexpectedly turned into the path of his host. He'd never met her before but had seen her picture many times. In his mind she looked like death warmed up, brought back to a simmer and then reheated a few times...

He smiled at her and introduced himself as Liz's husband. She didn't seem impressed but with all that cosmetic surgery it was hard to tell.

After the guests had imbibed some much-needed liquid heart-starters they seated themselves around the table for a catered four course meal. The editor, of course, sat at the head of the table giving all the impressions of being a benevolent host.

Silent waiters appeared with *'assorted bruschetta with fresh seasonal toppings - tomato & basil, roasted eggplant & feta, grilled zucchini & ricotta.'*

The entree was an *'Asian-inspired chopped salad with grilled chicken, sesame dressing, and crispy wonton strips'.*

During the main course of *slow-cooked pulled pork tacos with pickled onions, cilantro crema, and avocado salsa,* she kept referring to someone called Dunald Tramp. It was most disconcerting. Ray spent a lot of the main course trying to work out whether this was caused by some obscure regional accent or if it was done deliberately as some form of joke or test. Ray turned to Liz at one point and whispered, "Sorry, I'm really having trouble with her accent. Did she say he was appealing or appalling?"

Liz gave him one of those looks.

He got really stuck on the part where, if it was a regional accent, where on Earth speaks like that? He couldn't think of anywhere. He knew places like the north of England where *'lawyers'* and *'liars'* seemed interchangeable and consequently, he missed most of the important and interesting stuff.

He drifted back into the wider conversation. Something about only eating food grown by vegans and conscientious objectors. He drifted back out.

As he looked around the table, he saw a collection of people polishing their favourite topics, regrets and disappointments from the past. Each seemed determined to talk about theirs, while giving the minimum socially acceptable amount of reciprocity.

To his left, he heard someone say "Have you seen Spot, the Boston Dynamics robot dog. It looks like four one-legged riverdancers carrying a coffin."

"Oh no, don't get her started", Ray thought.

"River dancing. What's that all about?" said Liz disdainfully.

Too late.

"Dancing in a river? Who does that?" "Is it an interpretive dance representing someone trying to keep their head above water?" "Is that why they bob up and down all the time?" "... and why can't they put their arms up and wave for help?"

He'd heard it before.

He was suddenly distracted by the strangest cat he'd ever seen as it graced the room with its presence. It was completely hairless and knew how to make an entrance.

"Wow! A Mr Bigglesworth", Ray blurted. "What an amazing looking cat. What's its name?"

"I called her "Wrinkles"... after my Nan", said the editor, without a hint of irony.

Ray was unsure whether to laugh or make a comment. He let it slide. "She's a naturally hairless cat, isn't she?"

"Yes. Yes, she's a Sphynx cat."

"Wrinkles" the cat jumped onto the editor's lap and she clutched it closely and squeezed over affectionately, making the Dr Evil parallel clearer.

Pet or hostage of another species, Ray wondered, it's a fine line.

The conversation moved around, covering topics like the annual cull of the Darwin award candidates and why people whistle when they pick up something hot.

Liz encouraged Ray into doing his party piece. A sign language interpreter's translation of Gordon Ramsay forgetting to put on his oven gloves as he picks up a hot pot. It always went down a treat. It did again.

It was that sort of a night.

Later in the evening as the remains of the dessert of *'Mini baklava pastries with pistachios and honey syrup'* were being taken away and replaced with cheese platters, wines and coffees, the conversation drifted into things related to work and their award, Liz nudged him and said, "You look a long way away. What were you thinking?"

He flushed.

He'd been thinking about the time he was waiting for Liz at the pool, watching the elderly women's class swim up and back. It is incredible how slow they can go, he thought. Then there was *'that'* moment when he could see all the old ladies line up as a gigantic real-time Frogger game.

He became hypnotised as he noticed how a couple of particularly large ones were nicely spaced, then it was a big jump to get to the ones pushing their floating devices. He caught himself holding his breath as a perfect alignment occurred. He could see it magically line up before his eyes. Race to the other side of the pool on the backs of a bunch of elderly women. What was he thinking?

It would work though.

Hmm... Tempting.

The two sides were competing internally. It would work. It would be legendary vs how much trouble do you want to be in. This is one of those decisions where you get to voluntarily decide the height of the shit you are going to jump in.

"Nothing dear, not thinking anything."

She gave him a look that said she didn't believe him, but let it go.

As the party started to drift apart, Ray found that he'd once again inadvertently stood beside Liz's boss, the editor and host. He frantically wracked his brain trying to think of something to say. He knew there was some big deal about her having lots more plastic surgery, so he thought he'd be polite and asked when she was going in for it.

"I had the surgery 6 weeks ago", she said, looking at him as if trying to identify him by genus and species.

“Of course”, Ray tried to sound confident, “you must be very pleased” and hurried off.

“I s'pose she'll want her money back”, he said conversationally in the car on the way home.

Liz looked at him in one of those ways. This Botox stuff makes it very difficult to read expressions. Liz had only recently tried it for the first time. The intensity of the glare seemed to be the main thing... and a bit of a protruding jaw.

“Are you upset about something?”

“Yes.”

“Is this one of those times when your yes means no.”

“No.”

“I nearly died when you said that to her”, Liz unloaded, “What were you thinking? Couldn't you see that she looked different?”

“She always looks weird”, he countered.

“Oh God, she is going to make me pay for that”, Liz groaned.

“Sorry. I didn't do it to make things worse even though that is the outcome”, Ray half apologised.

“What can we do to make it right?”, he asked sincerely.

“Nothing right now”, Liz said gloomily.

Ray fell silent and thought, “Well, I didn’t have high expectations for the evening. I mean, I wasn't expecting a religious experience or anything, but it sure brought hell to life for me.”

He smiled at his own joke.

| 23 |

The knock on the door

Monday Morning

Two nights later, a storm lashed the house, pelting it with wind and rain but by dawn it had all blown away revealing a stunning and beautiful day. The sun beamed through the window and lit the room in a golden glow.

Liz woke up and thought, "How beautiful. I love living here."

With Ray away, this seemed a perfect day to play outside.

A walk, a bike ride? A swim? Some gardening? Maybe just coffee or lunch? It was a day off and she felt like relaxing.

As her eyes drunk in the scene, she noticed that the golden light was highlighting and amplifying every mote of dust in the entire room. Every mark on every window and surface.

My God, the place is filthy, she thought horrified.

How did I not see all that before?

It's an illusion of the light, she told herself. It happens when the seasons change.

It didn't help. Some vague memory surfaced of Quentin Crisp circulated around in her head, saying "There is no need to do housework at all. After the first four years it doesn't get any worse. It's all about not losing your nerve and starting to clean." Not helpful, she thought.

She grabbed her dressing gown, put on her slippers and headed for the laundry cupboard. Her head was starting to fill with how long this was going to take as she kept adding items to her to do list. This was going to take hours. At least until lunchtime. With her head swimming from the change of plans, her train of thought was interrupted by a loud and determined knock at the front door.

Tying her dressing gown tightly around her she looked through the peephole. It was a policeman.

???

She opened the door and asked, "Can I help you?"

"Excuse me madam, we're just doing house to house calls to see if you noticed anything out of the ordinary last night. In particular, next door. Did you notice anyone coming or going, between last night and this morning?"

"Which side?"

"Number 42."

"Why? I don't think so. I didn't get home until after 7 and my husband is away at the moment."

"I see. Did you notice whether the lights were on?"

"I'm sorry. I really didn't take any notice."

"What's happened?"

"We're trying to work that out at the moment. Your neighbour's husband and son have been reported missing."

"Oh no, poor Carol. I only saw them a couple of days ago. Everything seemed fine. They're a wonderful couple and the boy is delightful."

"Well, if you think of anything later, please contact this number". The police officer handed over a small card. On one side it said in large letters *'Missing Person Coordination Centre'* and a 1800 contact phone number. "Thank you."

Liz closed the door and leant against it, stunned. What on earth was that all about? She made a mental note to call in and see Carol later and offer her support. Oh, I have a bad feeling about this. She picked up her phone and called Ray. No answer. It just went straight to voicemail. He was probably in one of his meetings. Give me a ring when you can, our neighbours Eric and Simon have gone missing.

| 24 |

The interview

Wednesday Afternoon

Liz arrived early for the interview and settled into a comfy chair in the lobby. She gathered her equipment around her and waited, a bit nervously.

A tastefully dressed and manicured woman introduced herself. "Call me Angie", she said with a warm smile, "You must be Liz".

After briefly sizing each other up, Liz suggested they adjourn to the private room in the hotel her editor had booked. It was a small conference room with a large table, a breakout area and two large chairs with a coffee table in between. They settled into the large chairs.

"My editor said that you agreed that I can record this session but only audio", Liz asked, "Is that still okay?".

"Sure", said Angie, "just no pictures."

Liz studied Angie closely. About 30, she thought. She looked like so many professional women of that age. Well-dressed, well-groomed and an air of efficiency. The make-up, the clothes. Nothing was overstated or cheap or slutty. She wasn't a glamour-puss but she was an attractive woman. She reminded her a bit of her accountant.

"Okay, let's get started. Firstly, thank you for agreeing to the interview. I'm sure it will be a great help. I understand that my editor has already told you what she's looking for and that you can give me some perspective. Can you tell me a bit about yourself for background?"

"All right, but I don't want to make this about me," Angie said firmly.

"I am 29 years old, not married. I've been a lawyer for 3 years and started as a sex worker while I was studying for my degree. I was adopted and my adoptive parents died when I was in my mid-teens, so I had to put myself through uni. I was really struggling financially while watching others have such an easy time, wasting their parents' money. It was important to me to complete my degree but I just wasn't making it on the sort of work I could find."

"A girl I shared rooms with mentioned another way and introduced me to a club owner who used topless waitresses. The money was three to four times what I was making and soon I was doing four or five shifts a week. One week I had a tsunami of bills. My car broke down, my rent went up and my credit cards were already maxed out. My friend noticed I was distracted and distressed and mentioned there were other ways to make some quick money."

"I suppose my story is very similar to many. I just did it to pay my bills and thought I would only do it once. Of course, it doesn't really work that way. I spent a few hours with a nice man who talked a lot and yes, there was sex but it didn't really feel that different to some dates I'd been on. I only did it once and thought, that was it. The bills got paid and I went back to being a topless waitress four hours, five nights a week and continued my degree. Then a series of unfortunate events led to me being short of money again. It was harder the second time but it was relatively easy work and I could earn in one night what it took nearly all week to earn any other way I knew how."

They talked for the next three hours and Liz found that she was hypnotised by this woman. So strong and yet she thought she caught glimpses of fragility and rage.

Liz was starting to see a new picture emerge as she began to realise the crossover in services that are supplied by a psychiatrist or psychologist and the sex worker. Their costs are in a similar range. If sex on average takes three to thirteen minutes, then there is still lots of time to talk about yourself and your troubles to someone that you have paid to listen. She wondered which produces the best result.

They agreed to meet again in a fortnight to follow up, said their goodbyes and Liz watched her walk away.

The meeting had unsettled her for some reason that she couldn't quite explain.

| 25 |

Edward Andrews

Wednesday Evening

Edward Andrews looked up from his desk at the blinking light on his private phone line. He picked up the phone and said, "Yes?", in a way that made it a question.

The voice at the end of the line said, "It's done."

"Good. Were there any complications?"

"In a way. There were no witnesses and she is definitely dead but she didn't die from the initial impact of the car. I had to run over her to make sure. I've taken the car to the scrap yard as you asked and it's been crushed. There's nothing recognizable left."

"Is there anything else?"

"No, the job is complete. You can send through the remainder of my fee."

"I see." said Edward slowly.

He reached over to his computer and tapped away for a few minutes.

"It's done. Thank you. I hope you will take this in the spirit it is intended, but I hope we never have to see or hear from each other again. Goodbye." He hung up.

"Well, that takes care of that."

He sat back in his luxurious chair and probed the feelings rushing through him.

He'd never arranged for anyone to die before. It was a strange mixture of feelings. There was an exhilaration but also an emptiness that he couldn't quite place. She could have completely brought him undone. He briefly considered hiring another hitman to knock off the last one, just to be sure. That was probably just being silly and unnecessary. Would he have to hire another hitman to knock him off too. How far do you go?

He wondered, is that what's called an infinite regression?

With Angie taken care of, business could return to normal and he'd have to find someone to replace her. It was a shame. He'd enjoyed their times together.

| 26 |

The Editor makes her deal

Wednesday Evening

The editor sat down heavily and remembered back to the days when she would have lifted a beautiful old scotch to her lips while she plotted and schemed. Ahh... the good old days.

Bloody doctors.

She had one anyway. One shot and one for sipping.

She consciously focussed on her breathing and gathered the cyclone of thoughts in her head as she started to arrange them in broad priorities.

The highest priority is *'don't get caught'*. That's really important.

She stared intently at the document in front of her. She'd received word through her contacts that somehow, Angie was dead and now she was looking at a document that shouldn't exist. This was Angie's insurance. A list of her clients with dates, times and payments.

The list had the potential to be both dangerous and explosive. She knew nearly everyone on the list and its publication would certainly affect a few Christmas dinners and family get-togethers.

A few lawyers would do all right too. The list could never be published. There was far more value in it not being published.

She knew she was going to have to play a very dangerous game with some ruthless and powerful people but didn't really have a choice. Somehow, others would find out.

Could she let each of the names on the list know that it had come into her possession and that she'd suppressed it?

'*Keep that in mind next time I need a favour*' sounded like a plot line for an appalling Godfather sequel. There was also no guarantee that it would work 100%.

So, the dilemma was, she had a list of four names, addresses, meeting times and payments which if any of them knew existed, they would want it destroyed but, if she destroyed it without them knowing it had been destroyed they may still come looking for it or her. She may be able to use it as leverage but it also may completely backfire. She needed to speak with someone who would speak truth to her. Who?

The whisky was starting to work its magic.

She was nearly always surrounded by more yay-sayers than nay-sayers and she would have preferred Leo-sayers but... you can't always get what you want as Mick Jagger had pointed out. This was an unfortunate turn of phrase because now that line just kept going round and round in her head. '*You can't always get what you want.*'

Then she had a brainwave. I'll get Liz to do it. Liz was her least experienced journalist. The chances of her solving anything has to be remotely small. ...and it can be done under the umbrella of '*caring for my staff*'. They really got stuck into me over that last thing. She couldn't see what the problem was. Apparently, that was the problem.

"I'm still a genius", she thought madly.

| 27 |

The Hitman

Wednesday Evening

The hitman heard the phone call end.

"Prick."

The people I have to deal with, he thought. Just as well he paid.

Some people are just so… his thoughts trailed off.

It'd not been his best work. She'd seen him at the last minute and very athletically tried to jump out of the way. He only clipped her. It knocked her out but she was still alive. He'd quickly backed up and ran over her still body. That time there was no doubt.

He'd taken the car straight to the scrap yard and watched the car go through the big crusher. It was completely unrecognisable.

He glanced at his watch. He should try and get some sleep before his early morning start but he was still on an adrenaline high. It was hard to ignore the fact that it had happened again. He'd been unlucky… again.

Why do things never go smoothly?

It really was a repeating feature of his life. Extreme good luck and extreme bad luck. He knew that he was accident prone and always had been, even as a child. He just may be the *'Jacques Clouseau'* of the hitman world, but with careful planning he could usually overcome it. He thought back over his recent work.

That last one should have been so simple. He just had to break into a house and set a toaster as an electrocution trap. He even had a key to the place. It should've only taken a few minutes. In, out and on his way.

He'd decided to use an electric bike for the job. Powerful and silent, it was perfect. They were so common nowadays that it also worked as a very good disguise.

It had been a beautiful day and the warm wind felt great on his face. The intoxicating fragrances of honeysuckle, jasmine and gardenias filled the air. Hmmm. Beautiful.

It was nearly all downhill from where he'd parked the car, with a great final hill. He freewheeled the last two hundred metres and pulled into the alley behind the back of the house at about thirty k's an hour.

The two dogs who believed that they'd found a nice quiet, safe place to engage in a beautiful, consensual and non-binding sexual experience, couldn't have been more surprised than if an army of cats just stormed in from every direction demanding their immediate surrender or castration.

In the brief moment when both he and the dogs came to fully appreciate their situation, there was just enough time for the dogs to separate, causing considerable pain and possible permanent damage to both, as the bike dissected the air that they'd occupied only a fraction of a second before. The surprise of not hitting the dogs completely threw him and he careened into the fence in a manner best described as *'undignified'*.

As he came to a rest, he knew he'd hurt himself. The streaming blood was one clue and the numb feeling in both legs was the next. Before he had a chance to assess his injuries and see how many limbs still worked, he became aware of the dogs again. The dog's surprise at not being hit had now turned to pain, bewilderment and nasty thoughts as they both rounded on him, staring and growling in a very unfriendly way.

Without checking with his legs first, he was somehow standing, unentangled of the bike, and sprinting like a mad thing pursued by two dogs who had clearly identified him as the reason for their *coitus interruptus.*

In half a dozen strides he'd reached the side gate and managed to clear it in a single leap, something he'd never done before in his life. As he hit the ground on the other side, he heard both dogs hit the gate at the same time.

"Please God, let it hold. Let it hold."

He backed his way up the path fumbling in his pockets for the key. He had the key in the front door when the dogs started running up the path. "Oww shit. They've found another way. Typical. There must be holes in the fences everywhere."

He just got in the front door and slammed it shut as he heard both dogs slide on the slippery porch and crash bodily into the door. The sound contained both the dog's bodies hitting the wooden door and the sound of all the air in their lungs escaping in a single compressed burst.

Doof!

"I hope that really hurts", he thought loudly.

He looked down to survey his wounds. "I have to sit down", he thought. "My heart is going to burst out of my chest soon."

After a brief inspection he'd satisfied himself that there was no major injury. Just scratched and grazed. A bit of bark off. Some skin off. No need to mention bark really.

What a schmozzle! He'd lost his transport and could potentially start dropping blood everywhere. Of all the scary things he'd done in his life, retrieving that bike was right up there with his biggest career adrenaline rushes. Those dogs were big, they knew who he was and were very capable of keeping a grudge.

While that one had been bad, he'd still done the job. On time and without further incident which he thought was very lucky. That's the issue. Lucky and unlucky at the same time. Maybe it's just when animals are involved. He found himself shaking his head from side to side as he remembered that time with the cat.

Again, it should have been so simple. A developer wanted an old lady, who was refusing to sell her property to meet with an accident. One old lady. How hard can that be? No one had mentioned the cat. On reflection, even if they had mentioned it, he wouldn't have thought it could cause so much grief.

He'd entered the house just after midnight on a very dark night and walked gingerly and noiselessly into the lounge room.

It was quiet. His ears strained to hear any sound. It was some moments before he realised that he was holding his breath and he exhaled all the air that remained in his lungs in a single breath.

The sound woke the cat sleeping in the kitchen. He turned one eye on the intruder and spent a moment sizing him up.

As he began to refill his lungs with air, he became aware of the cat. It was a very large black cat and it was moving towards him in a strong purposeful slink. In his mind, the cat took on panther-like qualities. A mini Bagheera.

The cat slinked forward until it stopped about a metre or so away.

He realised that he was sweating and holding his breath again. His mind raced to food. Did he have any food? He mentally went through his pockets. There was a half-eaten burger in his jacket pocket from earlier in the day. He slowly reached into his pocket, never once taking his eyes off the cat. Bingo, it was still there. Pretty gooey and runny but with luck that's exactly how the cat likes it.

He broke off part of the burger and threw it in front of the cat.

The cat eyed it with suspicion, bent down and sniffed it. That was the moment. He realised in a flash he had his steel cap boots on. He could line up the cat like he was about to punt him through the goals to win the grand final.

The plan was good in a lot of ways, but conversely there were a few flaws. The first flaw was that if it'd been a dog, it would have had a much higher chance of success. Mainly because dogs are more stupid and react slower than cats. The second was that he was attempting to be quiet and not draw attention to himself and thirdly, who thinks kicking a cat is a good solution to anything?

The cat saw the boot coming at the moment before the last moment before the boot would strike. During this moment the cat had time to jump vertically in the air, thereby dodging the boot while extracting and extending every claw, fang and talon.

In this pose the cat attacked the extended right leg starting just above the Blundstone boot and continuing to his head where he turned around and ran back down the other side. The cat managed to achieve all this before the overbalance of the kick that'd hit nothing turned the unlucky hitman into a crumpled and twisted heap with a trail of scratches from head to nearly toe.

As he hit the ground, he was perfectly positioned to see the cat land gracefully in front of the burger and begin to eat.

"Owwww. I mean Fuck!" He bellowed and began making a series of crow impressions. "Fark, fark, fark!"

He went silent as he heard footsteps from another room and tried to pull himself up wincing involuntarily.

"Who's there?", asked a concerned elderly female voice.

He said nothing, while he tried to figure out what to do and how he could make himself invisible. He couldn't run and the cat was now between him and the door. He didn't want to tangle with that cat again.

"Who's there?" She repeated a bit more determinedly. "I've got a gun you know."

"Uh oh", he thought, "She might be worse than the cat."

In a fit of madness he dived for the door, startling at least one of the nine lives from the cat, opened the door and started running. The wall exploded behind him. The stupid bitch really had a gun and had tried to shoot him.

He didn't know at that stage that she'd never fired it before and the gun's recoil flung her back into the kitchen where she knocked herself out on a kitchen cupboard and died shortly after, completing the task he'd been sent to do.

Lucky and unlucky. Maybe he just wasn't cut out for this sort of work.

| 28 |

Reflecting

Wednesday Evening

Writing up her notes on the interview, Liz kept having a nagging feeling that she just couldn't place. She finally had the epiphany when she worked out the year that Angie was born. It was the same year that she'd given up a child for adoption. She'd pushed it out of her mind for so long now, she'd stopped looking at women of the same age.

Her daughter could be this old now. Even though it was just a coincidence, it started a melancholy tailspin. What if something similar had happened to her daughter? That's the problem, your imagination. All the what-ifs. As far as she knew, no one knew about it. She'd never told her mother or family members; she'd just gone away *'travelling'* for a year and given birth in a community hospital on the other side of the country. Her best friend was the only one who knew and she'd died nearly 15 years ago from some rare complication in a routine surgical procedure.

She really missed her. Her friend Sarah had been a gamer. On that final day she'd beaten all of her previous high scores on several pieces of medical equipment. She smiled wanly. She would've liked that one.

Ray never knew and she felt guilty about not telling him. She'd fantasised about a random knock on the door or phone call for a long time but eventually that happened less often and now she was too embarrassed and guilty to surmount the shame.

She'd never told the father of the child either, telling herself that it was for the best.

Reflecting on the whole situation had left her feeling flat. She wondered again whether she'd done the right thing. It'd seemed so grown up and in control at the time and she found herself deeply lost in thought.

I wonder where my daughter is right now?

Her imagination tried to fill in the blanks and she oscillated between being in a happy home with a loving partner to someone with Angie's story but without her strength and determination. What if she was lost? Not knowing why she was abandoned. Thinking that she was never loved.

She tried to pull herself out of the spiral but meeting Angie had completely derailed her. She was back in a cloud of self-doubt and confusion.

What if she'd done the wrong thing? Her life would have been so different. The flood of emotions overwhelmed her and she slid to the floor as tears and strange noises flowed out of her.

She wasn't really aware of how much time had passed while she was on the floor. It felt like an hour and left her drained and extremely sad. What am I going to do? Ray will be phoning soon and I'm not going to be able to pretend that nothing is wrong. He'll know and he'll worry. She really missed him at that moment and wished he could hold her. She decided to send a text message.

'I'm not feeling great, so I'm going to bed early to try and shake it. Talk tomorrow Xxx'. That would give her some time to think.

She spent the next few hours typing, doing her version of automatic writing. Trying to get her thoughts and feelings out and in some sort of shape. The word count told her that she'd typed three thousand words in three hours. It felt better but feeling good about it, still seemed as far away as before.

She went to the bathroom and looked at herself in the mirror. She looked terrible. The tears had destroyed her makeup and she realised that she looked like a cross between Alice Cooper and Robert Smith of The Cure if they'd been caught in torrential rain.

A joke. She realised it was the first funny perspective she'd found since disappearing down the melancholy gurgler. It had always been her strength. Finding a joke or funny perspective had made life more enjoyable and she was usually pretty good at it. Why had it failed her for the last few hours? Was the basic truth... this just wasn't remotely funny.

Then she remembered being told about God's sense of humour. Ray used the expression when bizarre or tragic things happened. Seeing someone stub their toe usually brings out a laugh in everyone except the stubee. God's sense of humour is sometimes hard to get, especially if you are the stubee. Was there a way to find perspective and not get caught up in feeling sorry for herself, wondering about the daughter she didn't know and the cost of the decisions that she'd made?

She started the shower, stripped and got in, letting the hot water cascade over her. She stood there for a long time, trying not to think and resisting the urge to follow every thought that entered and flitted through her mind. She had mixed success. Sometimes the thoughts made her angry and sometimes they just stripped away all her sense of self-worth and sometimes she could let the thought slide by without examining it. She kept telling herself, it's just a thought. I don't have to believe it. I don't have to act on it, I don't have to fight it. I can let it pass through." The thoughts that she couldn't resist, she clutched and examined like precious jewels. Perversely fascinated by facets that screamed out to be examined in minute detail. She felt helpless to resist.

After some time, she snapped out of the gloom and kept turning down the hot water until her body was forced to triage and concentrate on the cold water rather than her internal ruminations. It worked for a while. It had certainly helped the iceman, Wim Hof.

She got out of the shower, dried off, lay down on the bed and drifted off to a restless but exhausted sleep. Her dreams were complex, emotional and exhausting. Twice during the night, she woke with a start and once she cried herself back to sleep.

Liz woke the next morning with the clear understanding that she needed to talk to Angie again and that she was going to need some help to get through this. This thing she thought she had a lid on, had demonstrated very clearly that she did not.

Arriving at the office early, Liz looked up Angie's number from her notes and then at her watch. It's too early to ring, I'll try about lunch time. She decided to get stuck into some work to distract herself. She checked emails and lost herself reviewing a new sci-fi comedy book about AI and a time machine.

Around lunchtime, she dialled Angie's number. It went straight to message bank.

Liz left a short message asking her to return her call, wrote a quick note updating her editor on her meeting with Angie and went to lunch.

She walked to the park and sat alone in the crowd with her thoughts, vacantly not noticing the passing parade of people. Usually she enjoyed *'people watching'*. She liked to play a similar game to Ray and try to imagine what was going on in people's lives.

Not today.

| 29 |

They bought it!

Thursday Morning

Ray danced out of the office, trying to maintain some sort of composure, while all he felt like doing was grinning from ear to ear and bursting into song.

They bought it! They bought it!

Fighting the urge to click his heels together, he walked jauntily past the reception desk, smiled broadly at the receptionist, thanked her and continued out into the lobby. The world looked sunny and cheerful.

Oh, there will be some celebrating tonight. Once clear of the building he got out his phone and called Liz.

As soon as she answered, he gushed, "They are going to buy it! They are going to buy it! This time next year we'll be millionaires, quoting Del Boy from one of their favourite TV shows.

Are you there?

"Liz?"

"Did you hear? They want to buy it!"

"Liz?"

A strange, strangled voice said… "she's dead, I just heard, Angie is dead, she's dea... and broke into hysterical sobbing."

Ray's heart skipped a few beats.

"Wha?"

"Who?"

"WTF is happening?"

| 30 |

Travelling, not knowing

Thursday Evening

Ray boarded the plane frantically trying to keep calm. What was he coming home to?

Liz sounded in a terrible state. Would she harm herself? He didn't think so but he'd never heard her this bad.

The bottom had obviously dropped out of her world in some way. Why hadn't she been able to talk about it? He'd tried to ring Liz's mother while he was travelling to the airport but it'd gone to message bank. He left a slightly incohesive message that would probably really distress her but that's just the way it came out. He really was worried. He'd asked her to make contact with Liz and find out more about what was happening.

What was going on?

She hadn't been this upset since he'd done unspeakable things in her dream. Liz had woken one morning and been furious with him. He hadn't done anything he knew of but the dream must have been so powerful or realistic that somehow, she forgot which one was our shared reality. It had taken her ages to settle down. In hindsight, that was also a clue.

He was at least eight hours away from home and still had another plane, train and taxi ride to go.

An insistent internal voice was trying to talk over the general chaos in his head and remind him that there was absolutely nothing he could do while he was on the plane. Worrying and fretting wasn't going to help. If anything, it would make things worse. He knew the truth and value in this but was unable to calm the deluge of thoughts and feelings that rushed through him. Was she suicidal? Would she still be alive? Who was this dead woman? Why did it mean so much to her if they only just met? The questions continued like an out-of-control train in need of a driver. This wasn't helping. He rummaged around in his mental toolkit for something that would help.

A flight attendant asked if he was alright and would he like something to drink?

"Yes, he was fine", he lied and "Yes, he definitely wanted a drink."

As he tried to sip, not gulp the drink, he continued rummaging around in his mental toolkit.

Mental vigilance. He remembered the idea from a short book called *'Kindergarten for Adults'.*

When being overwhelmed mentally, bring your attention back to the present by naming out loud the things around you. He took a deep breath and started to whisper what he could see.

"I am sitting in a plane in an aisle seat, the seats around me are all full. The person in front of me is talking to a flight attendant. The interior colours are variations of beige. The seat isn't that comfortable. There are some magazines in the cloth rack in front of me. There is a mixture of perfumes and deodorants that are quite overpowering. There is a woman to my left with a very strong perfume and a man one row in front and to the right who must have bathed in cologne. Is that what Lynx smells like?"

He didn't know. He didn't like it either. He felt anger and frustration rising in him.

Settle. Keep calm. These are small things. You need to keep your shit together to deal with the big important things when you get home.

He closed his eyes and tried to meditate. Nothing happened. That's the trouble with meditation. At the times you need it most, it's the hardest to do.

He took another deep breath and started to count backwards from forty.

Ahhh. The Silva Method.

He had to go back and start counting from forty, three times before he maintained the sequence down to ten when a noise in the cabin distracted him again.

It was a baby crying.

As hard as he tried, he just didn't seem to be able to put the noise out of his head.

He and Liz had been unable to have children naturally and after exploring various options had given up. It appeared to be a problem with Liz and even though the medical professionals had tried to explain, he got the impression that they just didn't know why and for some reason, as medical professionals often do, weren't prepared to admit it. It seems they are taught that it is a grave and fundamental error to show your humanity over your authority.

It'd been traumatic and expensive to find that out. He'd just come to accept the fact that he would never be a father. In a world of population explosions, nuclear bombs and environmental chaos, he rationalised to himself that, maybe it was for the best.

Other times he thought about how, on the tree of life he was a genetic cul-du-sac.

He thought briefly about his cranky French hating neighbour who also didn't have kids. Maybe he should mischievously ask him if he thought of himself as a genetic cul-du-sac? He smiled a half smile. It was the first time since the phone call that he'd made a joke. Not much of a joke, but still. It softened his mood as he stepped back from his troubles and just lost himself in the neutral feeling that the silly joke had created.

He was transported back to that time when he was a kid and the fat lady singer had moved in next door and he'd created a whole drama in his head. It was the first time that he'd experienced that kind of chaos of his own making. Silently, and all in his head.

When he'd finally snapped out of it and reflected, he could see that it was very dangerous. He'd never talked about it with anyone. No one had known what he'd been saying to himself. How often the thoughts had passed through his mind, circled back and gone through again.

He'd resolved then to construct ways to prevent it from happening again. The little book Kindergarten for Adults had provided some of the tools that he'd used for over twenty-five years now. Mental vigilance, the 8-minute rule, growing mastery and battery chargers were the main ones he used and relied upon.

He focussed on the 8-minute rule. The idea was simple. When you go down one of these negative pathways, see how long it takes before you notice. It is fair and reasonable to get pissed off or frustrated at times. People do stupid, insensitive and cruel things. Sometimes we even do it to ourselves, waking up with a bad case of the "Oh No's" or the "I can't believe I just did that" type of memory. These do need to be processed.

Just not for hours and days and weeks and months.

8 minutes was the trigger to remind you to be aware of how long you're processing and ruminating. 8 minutes is just an arbi-

trary amount of time. It really just means, don't over-indulge it. Don't go into a complete funk. Don't waste lots of your life on it.

When he'd been learning this, sometimes days or weeks could go by before he noticed. He thought about it like golf or running, you are really only competing against yourself. Try for new personal bests. 8 minutes is up. Time to move on.

He took another deep breath.

The passenger to his left nudged his arm on the shared armrest and said "Are you alright? You seem to be doing some deep and heavy breathing."

"Yes, thanks. I'm fine", he lied, "Just got a bit on my plate at the moment."

The passenger smiled reassuringly and returned to his Kindle.

Ray looked down at the Kindle trying to identify the title. He recognised Isaac Asimov's Foundation. It was one of his favourite science fiction stories.

"That's a great book," said Ray, "One of my all-time favourites. That first book contained some absolutely genius ideas."

The man looked up and said, "I re-read the first book every year or so at least once. I love how it makes me feel about life, humanity, the future and of course the value of knowledge."

"I understand. I won't interrupt. I'll let you get back to enjoying the genius of Hari Seldon."

The man returned to the story and Ray pushed back in his seat, took another breath and felt a bit better.

Ahhh. The worldview of Hari Seldon.

Things would be okay.

Whatever happened, things would be okay.

| 31 |

Seth Barlow

The Past

Life hadn't gone as planned for Seth Barlow.

He'd rarely connected with people and many had treated him badly. He didn't want to think of himself as a bad person. No matter what he'd said or done... or thought.

Isn't that what everyone tells themselves?

I'm not a bad person.

Even though I've lied and cheated and stolen, been greedy and lustful. Probably tried each of the deadly sins at some point. Some of them, he'd tried a few times. Some he really liked and enjoyed. Lust was still a favourite. Adultery was still very popular with many people as far as he could see. So was stealing and coveting. There was still lots of that going on. He didn't consider that he'd ever murdered anyone though he had killed some for work, but that's different. He was a hitman. The question had finally been answered. He'd gone down both paths, socio and psycho.

At 16 he'd run away to sea, fleeing an intolerable home life.

He got work on a fishing boat and found a new family in the crew. They'd welcomed him into their lives and introduced him to many new experiences.

Alcohol for a start. Lots of alcohol.

They seemed to live to drink and the sessions could be brutal, especially the next day. To his horror, the whole crew was killed in a car accident and he was suddenly alone again.

After that, he worked in a factory briefly until one afternoon he dropped some acid.

It fell off the forklift he was driving when the pallet broke. Those outside showers really are lifesavers. It had left a scar on his leg where he'd been splashed and had been his constant reminder every time he undressed or thought about wearing shorts, it's so important to watch what you're doing and know that sometimes, things can go wrong in a big way, a life changing way, in less than a second.

Seth Barlow may be a hitman but he had standards. Even though there was no universal code of conduct for assassins and hitmen, he felt that he conducted his business and private life to a high standard.

It was work he'd drifted into over a few years and now was his main source of income. He wasn't squeamish or sentimental about it. It was just business. Someone pays him to do a job. He does it. Simple. No muss, no fuss.

As he got better at it he noticed how easy it can be to just make something look like an accident. This was his preferred way. No guns or knives to get rid of. Setting up a number of these *'accidents'*, he'd spent quite a bit of time just observing the general public while preparing a hit.

This had revealed a part of himself that he never knew existed. He discovered that he really hated litter. Not just a bit. A lot. It really played to both paths and triggered his socio and psycho buttons. Even more, he hated people who litter. He *really* hated people who littered.

In his mind it was acceptable to kill someone who litters because they are saying, *'I don't give a fuck about anyone else on the planet.'*

He was just doing his job when he was a hitman but taking out litterers made him a defender of the planet. Over a few years it had become something of a hobby, a sideline, even a mission.

He spent a lot of time setting up these accidents making sure there were no witnesses and it provided an outlet for his creativity.

He would find the perfect spaces where there were no security cameras or surveillance devices. He'd position himself in such a way that he could see if any member of the public had a camera or phone pointed in his direction. At times he used very small-scale EM pulses to guarantee that there couldn't be a working camera in the vicinity. Mostly it wasn't necessary. Sometimes things got elaborate but only if he couldn't find a simple solution. One of the most elaborate so far had involved getting the target involved in a brawl which caused him to be hospitalised, and subsequently die through a mix up in medication. The part that he was most proud of was the tie that he'd sent to the target with a request to wear it to the event. That night it'd enabled him to be easily identified by the group that he'd arranged to start the brawl.

He never really liked the term hitman, assassin or murderer, even though he had been called them all. To him it was just a job. Not everyone can do it. Not everyone wants to. It's a bit specialised but it's still just a job.

He still had vacations and weekends and had to get food and clothes and places to stay. In that way he was still very human. There was another part of him that wasn't really anymore. He'd crossed over a line many years ago and now the line was no longer in sight. Even if he'd looked in his rear-view mirror with a telescope he wouldn't be able to see that line. He chuckled. He always took it as a good sign if he made himself laugh or chuckle out loud. I'm still human, he thought and smiled to himself.

The question of whether he was still sane, didn't really come up.

It was four months since he'd worked last. That job had needed six weeks to set up and everything had gone perfectly. That was one of the keys. Don't rush, don't hurry.

Now that he had a few quid tucked away and was used to a travelling lifestyle, he could be flexible if he wanted to pursue his sideline during his breaks or anytime really if the situation presented itself.

His campaign against people who litter had stepped up over the last few years. He hadn't over analysed it but it seemed to start with a long surveillance job where he observed a market square for nearly three months. Watching the day-to-day goings on, he found he was drawn to this one guy who for some reason inflamed him with his casual attitude to litter. This guy just didn't care.

He watched him day after day throw shit everywhere. This is a guy who gets in his car, notices how much crap is in it, decides to empty it, by tossing shit out his car window while there are three rubbish bins within two steps. All the crap is now laying in front of a sweet little old ladies stall and when she calls him out, he just laughs and drives off, with his middle finger out the window.

That first incident he saw made him memorable and so he watched him as a sideline to the surveillance he was doing and just mentally noted a few more things he did. This guy was one of the bad ones. Callous, vindictive and uncaring. The idea that he could build it into the job he was being paid for and remove this guy as well, started to form in his mind. It was just an inkling but it hung around in his head and by the time he'd completed the surveillance he'd decided that it was entirely possible to complete his job and remove this littering arsehole along the way. He gave it the same scrutiny that he brought to all his work. It would work perfectly. Two accidents rather than one. Not that much harder to do.

After that one went well, he noticed that there was a lifting of spirits in the market now that the idiot was no longer there. The camera feeds he'd been using, he monitored for the next 3 months and it was like the place came alive. It was inspirational.

From this omniscient vantage point watching all these people interact for six months, he felt that he'd changed their lives for the better by the identification and removal of a blight on their community. It made him feel like a god and he'd never experienced a feeling like it before. It was wonderful. He could have an impact on people's lives in a positive way. It had been a breakthrough moment.

As usual he waited a few months before taking on the next job making sure that his tracks had been covered. This time it was in a large building. He wasn't looking for another litterer but he stumbled across another one. This guy was a real pig. Once again, he didn't get distracted from the job, just noted a few things along the way. One thing he noted was '*Some people are easy to hate.*'

Again, two accidents instead of one. He still got paid. It was just planning, designing strategies and his normal stuff. When it happened the third time, he recognised that a pattern was developing and that he needed to acknowledge it. As he summarised it to himself, it made him feel great to do some good in a community that he has gotten to know, probably better than it knows itself. Plus, he was good at it... and it was economical. Two for the price of one.

He'd seen in the news that a woman had been knocked down in a hit and run and recognised the name. He'd been offered that job but he was still finishing up his current one. He would have been a lot more subtle than that. That would have been painful and there was no need for that.

He was surprised to be asked a few days later to clean up the situation. His employer was of the same opinion as himself, that this wasn't well done, leaving too much of a trail and that it needed to be cleaned up properly. He wasn't leaning towards the job and framing his negative response when some documents arrived.

He glanced at the first page. The containment included the hitman, a newspaper editor, a journalist, a police officer and the journalist's husband. He stopped and stared. Surely not.

It was the same name. Could it be him?

He stared more closely and then started to zoom in.

It could be. He was about the right age.

This was his childhood neighbour. His fondest childhood memories were from those times. One of the few people who'd treated him as an equal, even liked him, trusted him. He knew straight away that he had to get involved.

He sent his reply. He would do the cleanup.

A day later, he'd pieced together a fair bit of the puzzle. He'd identified all the people who were taking an interest in the hit and run and questioning the "accident" story. Most people had accepted that it was an unfortunate accident while he knew for sure that it wasn't.

He'd looked into the lives of each of them and was pleased to discover that Ray had done fairly well. He lived in a nice house with his wife of twenty years. He was running his own business that had just sold his first major product. He looked good but he could stand to lose a few. His wife seemed pretty fit but also seemed a bit stressed. The police officer was not married and seemed to be exactly as she appeared. A young career cop.

The editor was another story. This one was into everything and everyone. Her network was large and she used it continuously, like a spider working from the centre of her web. He'd also been given details of the contractor who'd created the mess in the first place. He knew him by reputation but they'd never met. He'd thought he was better than this. Maybe something forced his hand? He had feelers out for him and was confident he would find him soon. Sometimes it's easier for the police to do the legwork. If they can find the person, it's quicker and easier for everyone. Once he knew where he was, he could deal with him.

He found that he was curious about Ray. It was nearly 40 years since he'd seen him. He never considered himself sentimental or nostalgic but a strange feeling brewed up inside him as he thought affectionately about the happiest time of his life and Ray had been part of it. The simple fun they'd had. It was the only times in his life he'd had a friend.

| 32 |

The editor calls

Friday Morning

Liz woke to the sound of her phone ringing beside the bed. She noticed the time as she picked it up, realising that she'd slept-in. It was Sue Thomas, her editor's PA.

"Hi Sue."

"Hello Liz. How are you?"

"Okay, what's up?"

"Boss wants to see you."

"Did she say what for?"

"Not to me. She just asked me to make a time for you to catch up and it didn't have to be at work unless you were already coming in. She did say that she was prepared to go to your house, if you didn't want to leave it at the moment."

A flash of panic filled Liz. The editor in my house. NO!!!! She shivered. No. No. No.

Sue sensed Liz recoil and suggested, "How about meeting for a coffee or a meal?"

"Coffee sounds good."

"Okay. I'll send you the address and time."

"What's going on? Why is she being like this... sort of nice?"

"Who knows what goes on in that head of hers. She's aware that you've had your world rocked with Angie's death."

"It could be as simple as she was already in various amounts of strife with HR about her treatment of staff and she's had to do some courses on how to treat her staff better. Maybe she feels a bit guilty or responsible for sending you into that world. I really don't know., I'm just guessing. My advice would be to accept it. Whatever her motives are, she appears to have your back at the moment."

"Look Liz, I have to go but do you want to catch up for a chat or a coffee soon? You know I've got a good set of ears."

"Sure Sue, that sounds great", and hung up.

Liz met her editor at a small coffee shop with the big six people booths. The place wasn't busy and they had a booth to themselves. The flavours of freshly brewed coffee and breakfast pastries competed with rich chocolate, cinnamon and nutmeg. It smelt delicious.

A waiter, wearing an awkwardly fitting yellow and red uniform appeared and they ordered drinks and snacks.

"Okay", the editor began, "firstly I want you to know how shocked I was to hear of Angie's death. I know this has affected you deeply as she had a powerful effect on you as we discussed previously. Take a little time if you need to find your centre or come back and get stuck into work. If you choose to come back to work, I would like you to follow up on Angie's accident. Explore it. Do the investigative journo thing. I have a few names and numbers for you. I'd suggest that you start with the police officer who attended the crime scene. Reassure yourself through this process that it was just a very unfortunate accident and then you can put it behind you or if there is more to it, we can try and find out what really happened. She looked directly into Liz's eyes with a mixture of query and urgency."

"What do you think?"

Liz said slowly, "Well, I don't think it is any good staying at home ruminating and I would like to know what happened to Angie and who did it".

She paused and breathed in deeply through her nose, filling her lungs and making herself sit up taller in her seat.

"Okay, I'll start the investigative journo thing in the morning."

"I was hoping you'd say that because in a few minutes the police officer is going to arrive. I invited her to meet us here."

"That was presumptuous of you", Liz eyed her warily.

Olivia Clemens smiled wryly and nearly winked. At least Liz thought it was a wink. The editor's recent botoxing and cosmetic surgeries made it hard to tell.

"I know people. As in, I understand people and I have a very large network. This is potentially a powerful time of your life. How you work through this will shape you for years to come. I think you'll do really well. I see strength and character in you and you have many of the right attributes for investigative work. I've enjoyed watching how your mind works."

Liz tilted her head quizzically but said nothing.

"I want you to think of this as one of the most profound opportunities of your life so far. Pursue this conscientiously and it will lead to great things. You'll overcome some personal fears and demons and begin your journey to becoming a great investigative journalist. I have complete confidence in you."

"Now, I have to get going, there are lots of things happening at the moment."

"The police officer will be here in a few minutes. Give me a ring or send me a message later and let me know how things are progressing."

With that, she stood up, smiled broadly at Liz in a way that said, "I dare you to say no" and waited for a response.

Liz was struggling to find words after the pep-talk and barrage of compliments. Internally, she was asking herself, was the editor always like this? Are those courses really good... or is something else going on?

Liz smiled weakly and said "Sure... Thanks... I will, not really sure if that was the response that she was wanting.

"Aah, here's Officer Churchward, just in time."

"Hello, I'm Olivia Clemens, the editor of The Morning News, we spoke on the phone and this is Liz", gesturing towards her.

"Now, if you'll both excuse me, I have another appointment, so I'll leave you two to have a chat." Without waiting for a response, she flowed out of the shop in what one bystander described as a *'delightful mixture of pastel colours.'*

Liz and Officer Churchward introduce themselves again and the officer ordered a coffee and a donut. They made small-talk about the editor for a few minutes and they agreed that she is a hard person to say *'No'* to. They both laughed and shook their heads in wonder.

"Okay, Officer Churchward, what can you tell me about the accident?"

"Now all this is public information, she said, I don't have any extra details that I'm not s'posed to tell you."

"Okay" said Liz, setting her phone to record the audio.

"We got a call at 11:37pm reporting an accident at St George's Lane. I was in the area and sent out to attend. My partner and I arrived at 11:42 and there was a woman in the road who'd been knocked down and run over but the vehicle fled the scene. An ambulance was called but she was declared dead at the scene. There were no obvious skid marks or damage to indicate the car hit anything else. We've looked for video surveillance footage but so far haven't found anything of the actual accident although we do have footage from around the area that probably shows the car that did it."

"Door knocking hasn't produced any witnesses so far and we've had no calls from the public. It appears to be an unfortunate hit and run accident. Sadly, they happen more often than you'd think. An autopsy has been conducted and the results passed on to the coroner.

Liz vagued out during the next bit as the description became more graphic and the details were sending shivers through her whole body. It was taking all her concentration and muscular control to avoid barfing up her breakfast."

"The victim, Angela Murray, had eaten a meal a few hours earlier and there was no significant alcohol or drugs found. She appeared to be in good health and the cause of death was ascribed to blunt trauma to the head and upper body consistent with being hit and run over by a car travelling at a reasonably slow speed. Hard to tell initially but probably less than 30 kph."

"We currently have teams working through the footage trying to narrow down which vehicles it could possibly be. It must be one of them. Unfortunately, it was fairly busy and there are a lot to check. My boss was reluctant to invest lots of resources into tracking that car down but I persuaded him to allow me to spend a couple of days on it. He's aware that it was difficult for me, being first on the scene as she is... sorry was, very close to my own age and had such terrible head injuries."

"That's the current state of play", said Officer Churchward, "Do you have any questions?"

"Absolutely", said Liz emphatically.

| 33 |

The 24th floor of the Andrews Building

Friday Evening

Edward Andrews paced in front of the large window in his office, high above the city. The vague ceaseless hum of traffic was a muted symphony of strident horns and sirens. The kaleidoscope of lights and colours competed for his attention but he didn't seem to notice.

He was working on a major deal. His hostile takeover of an investment bank. This could be a valuable asset in his holdings but there were problems. He liked the idea of being a banker. He was fascinated with the concept of 'Fractional Reserve Banking' which was effectively a way to invent new money. His people had prepared four options so far and he wasn't satisfied with any of them.

A delicate sound broke into his thoughts. He picked up the phone and listened for a few seconds.

"I see. Thank you. Let me know if it changes", placing the phone back in its cradle.

Another new development. Somehow, someone knew about his relationship with the dead woman. Where could they get that information? Even though Angie had sworn she didn't, she must have kept a list of meetings and contacts.

It'd been reported in the press that the woman was a lawyer and hadn't been identified as a sex worker and maybe she wouldn't be. He could always leak it. Would it help or make things worse? It was probably better to stick with "no comment" for now.

If someone had a list of Angie's clients it would be prudent to make sure it doesn't ever see the light of day.

He called his assistant and gave him instructions. "Find out who is making enquiries, who they are working for and anyone else taking an interest in this. Let's see who and what we are dealing with here."

Edward Andrew's networks were extensive and so he felt that he could confidently expect a detailed picture within 24 hours.

He sent a message to his hitman, cursing him for his incompetence and telling him that he had 24 hours to clean up his mess, otherwise he would take care of the hitman himself. He'd tried to be as threatening as he could, this was getting serious.

| 34 |

The next Friday phone call

Friday Evening

Liz rang her mother as usual, said "Hi Mum" and burst into tears. She'd been crying on and off all day and was having trouble holding it together. She apologised and promised she would ring her again soon, when she was able.

Her mother seemed to understand and didn't push the issue, although Liz didn't give her lots of choice. No jokes tonight.

Ray arrived home later in the evening and just held her. At that moment, that was what she needed. She'd not felt that much affection for him in a long while.

He listened patiently as she told him what she knew.

Angie had been knocked down by a car, less than nine hours after they'd finished their interview. Nine hours. It just didn't seem possible.

She filled him in about the editor's proposal, meeting Officer Churchward and Ray offered to help in any way he could.

She suspected that she'd need some support to get through this and was grateful for his offer. She didn't feel the need to mention the other stuff just yet.

Ray said, "You definitely did the right thing by cutting your phone call to your mother short. I love her but she lives her life according to Anderson's Law and I don't think that's what you need right now."

Liz nodded understandingly. Anderson's Law was well known in her family. Her mother continually demonstrated that no matter how complicated a problem was, there was always a way to look at it that made it even more complicated. It seemed to be one of her super-powers.

No wonder she's drawn to atheism, thought Ray. Loving your family isn't a stress reduction exercise, is it?

They spent the rest of the night on the couch watching a movie, settling on the Ridley Scott movie *'The Martian'* with Matt Damon as the hapless astronaut. They'd been looking forward to it but neither of them could concentrate very well and they just snuggled up in silence, Liz eventually falling asleep with her head in his lap.

| 35 |

Officer Churchward problems

Friday Morning

Taking a deep breath, Officer Sally Churchward knocked, turned the knob and stepped into the office of her boss, Captain Tim Egan. He had a kind face and a reassuring presence. As she entered he looked up from his paperwork, his eyes filling with concern.

"Sally," he began, his voice soft and understanding, "I just wanted to see how you were doing", he said, gesturing her to a chair.

Captain Egan smiled sadly. "Seeing something like that can take a toll on even the strongest person", he said, his voice filled with empathy. "It's important to remember that we're not supposed to be immune to these tragedies. It's okay to feel the pain, to let it out. It's part of the natural healing process."

"Seeing a body that badly battered, about your own age, it's hard not to imagine it could be you. It's a lot to take in and process.

"So, how are you coping?" he leaned forward to emphasise his caring posture.

"Fairly good... so far", she began falteringly.

"It's not the first dead body I've seen although it was the most damaged. I've attended fatal car crashes that were less horrific. This was bad, from the point of view that you could really see the damage and a skull crushing is a terrible thing to view, it distorts the face and head so much.

If I focus on the image or allow it to stay in my head for too long, I want to retch. I've been fighting the urge continuously."

Captain Egan said nothing. His years of experience told him that he needed to wait patiently and silently for her to continue.

After a long pause, she went on, "To be honest it's caught me out a few times in unexpected ways. I went through a stage in the first few days, where my imagination was taking any person's head and superimposing it over the memory of what I saw. It completely threw me the first time as it was at a friend's daughter's birthday. I suddenly got a flash of the birthday girl's head crushed in. It was disturbingly realistic and chilling." She shuddered involuntarily.

"Have you spoken to one of the counsellors... or anyone else", he asked, his voice rising with concern.

"I was contacted by the editor of The Morning News who'd sent a journalist to interview the dead woman, Angela Murray, on the day she died. The journalist, Liz Barton, was quite traumatised by Angela's death and the editor asked for my help... you know, helping work through the trauma with her."

"Even though the editor is ultimately looking for a story out of all this, she does seem to understand that working through this is good for both of us and our mental health. Rather than bottle it all up, systematically working through what happened does seem to be helping us both."

"If it is alright with you I would like to continue working with them. I'm not passing on any information they can't get other ways and it is helping me by helping her, if that makes sense."

He looked down his nose, through his glasses, smiled benevolently and said "Of course, I understand."

Whenever Captain Egan did that look down his nose thing over his glasses, he reminded her of her own father. Sadly, now passed away and physically very different from her boss but he had the same habit. She understood at some level it's just one of those age-related things where the eyes become good at some focal lengths and not others. Somewhere in the back of her mind, vague recollections of the Mole from Wind in the Willows hovered around. She found it reassuring.

He said, "Courage is much admired in culture. It is both praised and rewarded."

"Everyone who does something courageous has done so, not knowing for sure that it will all work out and for some it doesn't."

"If it works and you survive, it is called courage. If it doesn't work, a coroner usually calls it death by misadventure. Keep that in mind."

"Things don't always work out. It's one of things that you find out the longer you serve as a police officer, the more times you will experience real life, where it didn't work out for someone, their families and loved ones."

They talked for another 15 minutes or so and then she returned to her desk to spend the afternoon completing some of the never-ending paperwork and finally knocked off a little after 4:00 pm.

After work she returned to her flat, opened the front door and was welcomed by her flatmate Jen's cat, '*Mr B*'. Sally and the cat had an on-again off-again relationship. If Jen was around, *Mr B* would completely ignore her but if Sally was in the flat on her own, the cat would graciously condescend to allow her to prepare food, be a scratching post or provide a space to be sat on.

Jen must be running late as *Mr B* was insisting that looking after *Mr B* was the top priority and was making lots of noises, rubbing up against her legs and trying to physically direct her into the kitchen.

She knew that it was simpler to just get it over with and grabbed a tin of cat food, upended it in the cat's bowl and refreshed the water. This didn't meet with *Mr B's* approval and he showed his disapproval by making more noises and putting more expressive pain and raw emotion into the 'meow' sound.

"That's all you are getting *Mr B*. Why don't you try it? It's good for you. It says so on the tin". She spoke to the cat in that anthropomorphising way that so many people do by talking in complete sentences.

Locking the cat in the kitchen, she went into her bedroom, took off her uniform and headed for the shower. It was a ritual that when she took off the uniform, she showered. It helped the psychological change from Officer Churchward to civilian Churchward.

Sally Churchward got out of the shower and dressed in her *'home'* clothes. She wasn't going out again tonight and so she dressed for comfort.

It was surprising that her flatmate wasn't home yet and she was starting to move from wondering to worrying. Jen was a theatre nurse at a nearby hospital and it was a good living arrangement as they both did shift work. Three to five days a week they each had the place to themselves but tonight they'd arranged to have a meal at home and catch up. Plus, it was Jen's turn to cook. They tried to share a meal at least once a week. It didn't always work out.

Her phone binged. A text message from Jen.

Bumped into an old friend and gone for a drink. Sorry. Can we catch up another night? PS I'll probably be late home. X (folded hands emoji, heart emoji)

Sally stared at her phone, wondering if it was a blessing or a curse?

With a blur of motion, her thumbs danced over the phone's screen. "No worries, I'm ready for an early one anyway. Have a good night. X"

"Okay, just me for the evening meal", she said out loud to no one in particular.

She returned to the kitchen and opened the fridge and peered in optimistically. Some sad looking vegetables in the crisper, some milk, yoghurt and other dairy products peered back. All opened and out of date. The rest seemed to be containers of takeaway food in different stages of some fermentation experiment. A microbial metropolis. She opened the freezer. There were 4 microwaveable quick meals. They had the nutritional value of sucking an icy pole stick but this could be overlooked by their virtue of being quick and filling.

While she waited for the microwave to finish, she emptied the contents of the fridge into a rubbish bag revealing how much the fridge really needed a good clean. The only thing left were some sample bottles of some brightly coloured flavoured spirits and a cask of wine left over from a small party when they moved in. They were from a promotion where gin, vodka and rum were put in trendy looking packages with a range of flavourings added. She looked more closely at the labels. Gin and blueberry bliss, vodka and chia-mazing, rum and raison d'etre. Sounded diabolical to her.

She settled in for a quiet evening in front of some mindless TV and went to bed around 10 o'clock. She heard Jen arrive home around 1am with the exaggerated shooshing and giggling of a drunk couple unsuccessfully trying to be quiet.

Jen had more friends stay over than she did. She also drank more and was more social and extraverted. She also made lots of noise when she was getting it. She tended to be rather noisy in the sack.

Sally Churchward wondered where she'd put her ear plugs, realising that the couple would be oblivious to her. If they thought that they'd gained entry to the flat without waking anyone, it showed just how unaware they were.

A rhythmic squeaking started.

Oh crap, that didn't take long, they're into it already. The sound of an IKEA bed that really needed tightening up filled the soundscape. What on earth were they doing? She wondered how long she'd have to listen to this unintentional percussive accompaniment to their impromptu nocturnal concert.

She reached for the ear plugs and inserted them snuggly in each ear. As she lay back down, she realised that they weren't working 100%, she could still hear the squeaking bed. Hmmm.

After being asleep for a few hours, she was now wide awake and staring in the darkness at the ceiling.

She tried to distract herself by going over recent events. She felt a strong connection to Liz and appreciated the bond that their shared trauma had delivered to them. That editor was another story. The first word that sprang to mind was '*psycho*'. Probably not technically accurate and more Alfred Hitchcock than the clinical meaning but it seemed appropriate. Something was definitely not right about her. She couldn't put her finger on it but something wasn't right. She eventually drifted back to sleep.

Sally woke the next morning with Jen shaking her. With her earplugs in she'd not heard her alarm.

"Wake up sleepyhead", Jen teased, "You nearly slept in."

Sally looked at her uncertainly as if trying to work out who she was. She removed the ear plugs and said, "What was that?"

"Morning Sally, look I'm sorry I didn't get home for our meal last night. Thanks for feeding *Mr B*".

Sally looked at her flatmate. She looked impossibly fresh and healthy. How does she do that, she wondered?

"I heard you come home about 1:00 am and then you had noisy sex for the next hour or so and then passed out. I had to put ear plugs in." That bed of yours really needs some attention, it shouldn't make that much noise.

"Sorry", said Jen, "I bumped into Matt Harding. Do you remember him from our housewarming party?"

Sally said nothing but screwed up her face to indicate that she couldn't remember him.

"Anyway, I have to run. See you tonight?", Jen asked quickly.

"Ahh, not tonight, Jen, I promised to catch up with that journalist I told you about."

"Okay, we'll talk soon", yelled Jen over her shoulder as she headed out the door.

| 36 |

24 hours later

Saturday Evening

Edward Andrews was seated at his desk when his assistant returned.

"What do we know?", he said impassively.

"The journalist is basically a newbie and has never done any serious journalism. It appears to be some sort of therapy for her as she'd only just interviewed the woman earlier that day and her death has shaken, rattled and rolled her."

"Her editor seems to have given her the job rather than go on stress leave, so from that regard, it is highly unlikely that she will get very far."

"What does she know so far?"

"Somehow, there seems to be a list of the dead woman's clients. It must have been some form of insurance. The editor seems to have a copy and I suspect there were also some police or high-ranking legal people have it too."

"My gut feeling is that there is probably someone on the list that the editor wants to protect and that's why she's done what she's done. The editor is very widely connected and is bound to know at least some of the people on the list. She may want to use it as leverage or for some other purpose."

"We've hacked the journalist's notebook and seen her notes and emails to her boss, the editor. She has written up her meeting with the dead woman and the police officer in considerable detail. They have a cop working with them too. As far as we can tell, she hasn't passed on any information that isn't publicly available but she was the first on the scene, is about the same age as the dead woman and has taken a personal interest in it."

"The journalist's husband is also helping them. He seems to be a self-employed inventor or designer. It's hard to work out from his website. He's just signed a deal to get one of his ideas developed. He seems to have some computer and design skills but nothing exceptional. He doesn't seem to have contributed much so far, just some moral support."

Edward Andrews reflected on the information and said, "It's important that we don't underestimate the power and luck of people who believe that God, truth or justice is on their side."

"Keep an eye on them and just make things a bit difficult for them for now. Usual stuff. The flat tyre, the broken washing machine, wallet or car stolen, things that require time and attention in their personal lives. Can we slow them down without showing our hand?"

"I'll get onto it. I'm sure we can find some candidates. Who do you want to target?"

"The journalist, her husband and the cop. The editor has too many resources to be played that way. She would just delegate."

"...and have a closer look at that editor, see if it's a physical list or purely digital?"

| 37 |

Surveillance from Barlow

Very Late Friday Evening

Seth Barlow's mentor was a man called Simon. He provided the bulk of his work and Seth assisted various operations within Simon's worldwide network and resources.

He'd only met him a few times and communications between them were usually left as messages.

Simon appeared to run some sort of a research agency which employed many private investigators, technical staff and the odd hitman and assassin. Whenever Seth received information from Simon, he always found it to be from a God-like perspective with an accuracy that far exceeded any single country's reach as far as he could see. He'd wondered occasionally how it was possible but was happy just to accept it. It was a mystery he could live with.

News arrived from Simon that the unlucky hitman was on the move and heading towards Ray and Liz's house. The countdown had started.

Seth Barlow ran through his options once more. He'd already considered this possibility and put measures in place to prevent any harm coming to Ray or Liz. The decision he was flirting with was, should he go in person? It wasn't necessary. The people he'd put in place were solid... but... he was curious to see Ray again.

He sent a message to the surveillance company he was using for this job. Expect an observer to join you shortly. He ran through his mental checklist, ticking off each item, grabbed his gear and headed out.

Joining the surveillance crew, Seth told them he was from another job which was now crossing over with this one. He didn't reveal that he was their employer. His target was heading to the target that this team was watching, to do something. Probably not good. We're not sure if he intends to kill them but it appears he's been backed into a corner and may be either desperate, stupid or just not thinking very well. That's what caused the whole mess in the first place. He'd not done a good job on the original hit.

The surveillance team explained their setup, made some adjustments based on the new information and settled in to wait.

An overweight operator who appeared to be encased in his chair seemed to appreciate some new company and was making his position clear to the newcomer.

"We're just the surveillance team. We don't do any action stuff. Other people do that. We just watch people and make reports. That's our job. We're not heroes."

"What's the status?", asked Seth.

"Everything's quiet in the neighbourhood. The cops are doing regular sweeps of the area and passing the house every hour or so at this time of night. Of course, they're focussed on the house next door. The hitman is being followed by trackers built into his boots, cap and underwear. The watchers are watching the watcher."

| 38 |

Edward Andrews gets a note from Simon

Very Late Friday Evening

Edward Andrews was standing by the window as he received a report that the hitman was on the move. His assistant knocked and came in holding a piece of paper. I've just received a message from an anonymous source. He looked bewildered. I'm not really sure where it came from.

It reads. "Simon says, stop trying to cover up your mess, you will have to face the consequences. This is strike two."

"Oh fuck, Well, that's that then", Edward Andrews said in a deflated, flat low tone. "We have to stop. It's over. If Simon says… it's hopeless."

He moved to his drinks tray and poured himself a large single malt scotch whisky into an elegant crystal tumbler.

"What do you mean? Surely, you're not serious. You're Edward Andrews, multi-billionaire. You have resources all around the planet. Who is this Simon and why are you taking it so seriously?"

He looked at his boss who'd stood tall and strong only moments ago and now looked crushed and broken. He looked somehow shorter, older, weaker. WTF?

Edward Andrews took a slow deep breath and then in the same low voice said," He basically runs the world".

"He what! How? He trailed off unintelligibly... Really? Why haven't I heard of him?"

"Hardly anybody has and he likes it that way. I've only met him once and it was when I thought I was the king of the world. Everything seemed to be going my way. And then I unwittingly interfered in one of his projects. I didn't know. I thought I was invincible and nobody better get in my way."

He paused, took another slow deep breath and then a deep gulp of his whisky.

"I had the best security I could buy and state of the art protection in the building that I own. This building. You know what the security is like in this building. It's world class. Better than some military."

"He bypassed the whole lot and came and had a talk to me in my bedroom on the 51st floor. My first awareness of his presence was when he placed a little clip thing on the end of my fingers. I'd been asleep and was instantly awake from the unfamiliar feeling. He was just sitting beside the bed staring straight into my eyes. I think I went to cry out or move. Not sure which but nothing happened. I seemed to be paralysed. I couldn't move, couldn't speak. His gaze never varied as I expressed what I could through my eyes. For some reason they still worked."

He tilted his head and looked at me quizzically.

"My name is Simon. As you have discovered, you can't operate your body or your voice at the moment. It is temporary but you'll remain like this until I am finished.

I am aware of your story and rise to power. You've done well for yourself. You appear to have been under the impression that you were at the top of the mountain and king of the world due to your recent successes."

"I am here to tell you that is not the case. All the resources you cherish so much and give you your sense of power, can be taken away from you like that." He snapped his fingers. The sound seemed unusually loud in the serenity of the room after his quiet voice. "There is nothing you can do about it. You thought you were playing with the big boys before but the actions you have taken recently brings you to my attention."

"Now personally, I don't really care whether you do well, live or die. It just simply does not matter to me. It does seem to be important to you."

"Now you probably thought that you were safe here in your inner sanctum. I am here to show you that is not true. I can get you anywhere and anytime I like and I'll demonstrate that to you tomorrow. I'm here to tell you that this line of investment is not for you. There are many other lines of investment that can perform better. I'll even suggest some if you like. The important thing to remember from my visit tonight is that when you go to work tomorrow, you'll have a revelation about the extent of my reach and you'll move your investment focus in another direction. Then you won't hear from me again. Unless you move in this direction again, attempt to find me or get in my way. I do believe that once can be an accident, but not twice and I don't give third chances. There is still a very large playground for you to play in. Just keep in mind who owns and runs the playground."

Another pause. Edward Andrews shook his head and shivered.

"And... what happened the next day?" asked his assistant disbelievingly.

My personal passwords for the highest level of my security and financial access was sent to me by courier on the back of a postcard addressed to the Security and Exchanges Commission."

"I took the hint. There were other things that I could invest in. I ordered my staff to change direction and abandon our previous plan. Within three minutes, definitely less than five minutes a phone call came through to my unlisted private number from a male voice which said, "Good choice. Try Arangain."

"Oh."

"I'd looked at them and couldn't really see anything interesting in their public material but I put a million dollars into them out of curiosity."

"You know what happened next. What a run. I couldn't really explain what happened. The guy could have killed me if he wanted. He cut through all my defences, seemingly effortlessly and then showed impossible networking and reach. He then passes on a tip which turned my original million into a billion. A 1000x increase. I figured that he didn't really mean me any harm. He had shown that he was happy for me to make money but to avoid some areas. What can I say? I respect that. I still have no idea who he is or what he does but he made me feel like a child being kindly guided by a benevolent but powerful parent."

"The more I reflected on what he could have done when he casually bypassed one of the best security systems on the planet. He shivered. I've been successful by picking and choosing my battles and this one didn't seem worth pursuing."

| 39 |

The Great Dane gets home

Friday Night

Liz and Ray were in bed reading. Liz was looking at social media on her tablet, while Ray was trying to read another classic on his Kindle app. He'd been trying to work through all those classic novels that he thought he should have read, or that he thought he'd read and couldn't remember. Tonight, he was trying to get through a few more pages of William Shakespeare's classic, Macbeth. For some reason reading classics made him sleepy and so he didn't get through a lot of pages until that soporific effect happened. He'd proudly never completed a single Shakespeare work. Never. He felt like the shepherd who never knew how many sheep he had because every time he counted them he fell asleep.

Unexpectedly and loudly, Liz's phone rang. They both jumped involuntarily.

Liz picked up and looked at the screen. It was the Great Dane. More than a fortnight had passed since she'd stayed with them.

"Hi Sofia, I'm just putting you on speaker, Ray's here as well", Liz spoke a bit more loudly while tapping at her phone.

"Hi Ray", said Sofia enthusiastically, "Thanks again for your hospitality. I really enjoyed my time with you both and apologise for anything I did wrong or misunderstood."

"There is nothing to apologise for Sofia", Ray joined in, "it was great to finally meet you."

"How was your trip home", Liz asked.

"Funny you should ask", Sofia answered, "a few strange things happened on the way home. I had to wait an hour and a half at the airport so I went looking for something to eat. I picked up a coffee and some sandwiches and found a seat by the window where I could look out on the tarmac and see various planes, ground crew and general airport activity.

I was happily lost in watching the scene when one of the ground crew vehicles ran into another one. All the suitcases went everywhere and the drivers of each vehicle were really upset with each other. They started yelling at each other and then a physical fight started up. Another ground crew joined in and soon it was on for young and old. Did I get that right? That's an Australian expression, is it not. *'On for young and old"*.

Liz and Ray chimed in, "Perfect Sofia, that's exactly right."

"Anyway", Sofia continued, "they'd lost all interest in luggage and were starting to beat the crap out of each other. Within minutes, security arrived and joined in. Somehow, they made it worse as the ground crews now combined and started beating up the security guys. My favourite bit was when one of the ground crew, a really big lad, laid out two of the large security guys just by hitting them on the top of their heads with his open hands. Their legs just collapsed underneath them.

Finally, some police arrived and arrested everyone. Ground crew, security guards and some unfortunate bystanders. The whole thing was over in about 15 minutes. Ground crew vehicles and luggage were just left wherever they'd landed or stopped."

"Just as I was thinking, well that was better than television, two police officers approached me and asked if I'd seen what had happened."

"I explained that I needed to catch my plane but was told that after what had happened, many flights would be delayed as there would now be a shortage of ground crews and security personnel."

"I explained what I'd seen, thinking that would be the end of it but they wanted a full statement from me."

"So, I'm looking out at the spilled luggage and odd drops of blood, pointing out what had happened where, when I recognised my own suitcase. I always put a very colourful scarf through the handle of my suitcase to make it easy to spot on those luggage carousels. Anyway, there it was lying on the ground amongst a pile of others."

"I said this to one of the police officers. I've just noticed my own suitcase. Who's going to get it?"

"They didn't know."

"Anyway, all this meant that my flight was delayed and consequently I would miss all of my connecting flights. The airline was very apologetic and paid for an extra two night's accommodation while my travel agent rebooked all my flights."

"It took a day to get all my flights reorganised but I finally arrived the next night in Singapore and went to collect my luggage. I'd been slightly delayed getting to the carousel because an elderly man in a wheelchair got into trouble on an escalator and all the people banked up behind as various people tried to get his wheelchair unstuck."

"Anyway, by the time I got there most of the luggage had been collected and as I watched the suitcases go round, I couldn't see my bag. There was an identical bag but it didn't have my scarf on it. I watched for a while and all the rest was collected and only this one suitcase was left. It looked like mine but it wasn't mine."

"I had that horrible sinking feeling that someone must've taken my bag by mistake. Sure enough, someone had picked up my suitcase by mistake. So, I pick up theirs and take it to the lost and found luggage claim place."

"This introduced the first of the language problems I faced. I think if you asked us individually, we would say that our English is fairly good. It gets a bit comical when you have multiple people trying to communicate in their second languages. Someone who mainly speaks Mandarin but has good English talking to a Danish woman who also thinks their English is good. The combination of accents is quite amazing."

"I explained that the suitcase isn't mine but mine is identical. Can they track down the owner while they're still in the airport? It was hard to explain and it took a while to get the whole concept across."

"They got security people involved as under their own guidelines I was presenting them with an abandoned suitcase which could have all sorts of implications. It could be a bomb, gas or some other nasty. That hadn't occurred to me before and I did shit myself for a while."

"Of course, I couldn't open the suitcase and the security people wanted to force it open as they are concerned that someone may have left it on purpose."

"They put it through an x-ray machine and get more alarmed."

"They take it to one side and try to open it somehow. All I heard was some mutterings followed by a shriek and then very loud bellowing and yelling."

"By opening it without the key, the protective inked dye packs had triggered, exploded and released a cloud of ink, covering the security officers in dark blue ink."

"Ignoring the distress of their colleagues, now that the case is open a '*clean*' officer is urged to look inside by their superior. They hesitantly reach a smaller case inside and a glitter bomb goes off covering her and the two blue officers in a cloud of sparkling glitter."

"The security people are now really upset and even though it isn't my bag, they are pissed at me. I was completely unmarked but the three security people are now blue, very shiny and not impressed."

"They make me wait for ages before two clean officers arrive and escort me to the security gate. You know I tend to have issues at airport security as I'm large, loud and nearly always set off metal detectors because I have piercings. Three quarters of Danish women do. I used to have both ears, nose, belly button and nipples until I realised what a pain it is to go through airports."

"Of course I set it off as usual. I really have no idea how those things work. One time it was the wire in my bra and once it was my surgical implant. I was part of an experiment at work where I had a subdermal microchip implanted between my thumb and index finger. It worked with a reader that could unlock doors and turn lights on and off. It was fun. A bit like having a superpower. It's painful to have to explain to people who don't speak your language that it has nothing to do with spying. It is just a university experiment."

"The customs officer thought I might be a smuggler because I was flying with no luggage and had a microchip in my hand. They thought I was smuggling sensitive information out of the country."

Liz's laughter grew louder and more frequent, swept away by Sofia's infectious humour. Sofia continued her tale of misadventures, painting vivid pictures of her chaotic journey,

When Sofia finally finished her story, they were all in stitches, their faces flushed with laughter.

"You always make me laugh Sofia," Liz said, wiping away a tear, "I needed that."

Sofia nodded, "So did I, Liz," she replied. "So did I."

"Anyway, I just thought I'd let you know that I got home safely and they've already announced the intention of holding another conference in 2 years time. I'd love to come and see you again."

"Sounds good Sofia. Let us know the details when you find out."

"Will do."

"Bye for now." The Great Dane rang off.

After Liz put her phone on her bedside table, they talked briefly about the Great Dane's visit. She'd been fun and they could see no reason not to do it again. Two years seemed like a long time away, but it felt okay to agree.

"By the way"", said Ray, as he put his tablet away, "I bumped into Carol from next door earlier at the supermarket. Pffft. It's hard to know what to say to her. We should have a BBQ and invite her over. Invite Gabe and Molly. What do you reckon?

"Sounds good"

Anyone else you would like to include?" Ray asked.

"Well, Carol has a friend Wendy staying with her. It might also be polite to invite that police officer I met through work. She's dealing with a lot at the moment too and I liked her. She seemed nice. "

"Okay, I like it", said Ray, "I was going to see Carol over the weekend to return that wet and dry vacuum cleaner. I'll ask her then, unless you want to do it? When do you reckon is a good time?"

"How about next weekend?"

| 40 |

A clue

Saturday Morning

The next morning Liz rang Officer Churchward for an update.

"Hi Liz, the forensic team reckoned that Angie was hit by a van or SUV, not a sedan or bike. There'd also been a breakthrough from the video surveillance footage and they'd identified all the vehicles that were in the streets leading to St George's Lane just before and after the time of the accident.

They'd identified all the number plates and traced each of the vehicle's owners. It'd taken some manpower to do it but they narrowed it down to 3 possible vehicles. They'd found one of them and he denied it. Vigorously. We're working on the other two now. It's highly likely that it's one of them."

"Anything I can print? Or research? Can I have the names? You know I can't print them." Liz scribbled furiously for a few seconds and then said "Thanks" and hung up.

She turned to Ray. "Okay, I don't know whether you got all that. They've narrowed it down to three possible vehicles. They've talked to one, who denied everything and they're tracking down the other two. I've got the names of who the cars are registered to.

"They are Roland Davis and a business called Edward Andrews and Associates. Ring any bells?" She looked hopefully at Ray.

"No, sorry", he shrugged, "I don't know the names."

The weird thing is that both these vehicles were reported stolen.

"Alright", said Ray, "Let's do some quick research and see what we can find about these people. I'll do Edward Andrews and Associates."

They each turned to their laptops and started tapping away.

After a few minutes Liz said, "Roland Davis seems to be a plumber. Runs his own business. An owner/operator sort of business. He has a website, which shows a work van and his apprentice or assistant. It looks like a husband-and-wife small business partnership. His Facebook page shows a couple of kids under ten, some animals or pets and the family doing things in the water.

All seems like a regular family. No obvious flags yet. Anything on the other one?"

Ray said, "This guy seems to have money around him. Some corporate role in finance or banking or insurance. I'm still finding my way. Seems to be involved in all those things. Can't find anything about a family yet."

"Do we know where they live?" Liz asked.

A flurry of clicks and swipes and Liz got there first. "Roland Davis lives in suburbia in a small family home. Google Maps shows a nice backyard, a second car in the driveway and lots of trees and plants."

"What have you found out about Edward Andrews and Associates?"

"Hmmm", Ray said thoughtfully, "Not so obvious. He doesn't seem to have social media accounts."

Ray tapped away some more. "Aahhh. He is on a board, which lists his address on the website as The Blue Sky Tower, aka The Edward Andrews and Associates Building. It's a big building in the city and to live there would be a multi-million dollar investment. Maybe it's just a postal address. Maybe its…" He trailed off.

Then he had an idea. "Maybe you should ring your editor and bring her up to date. She may know more about him." Ray suggested.

Liz agreed and rang her. After waiting a few minutes, she explained what they'd found.

"I know that building", said the editor and looked at the list of Angie's appointments and contacts.

"Okay Angie regularly visited that building and would see someone on the 24th floor. Someone called 'Gerald'. I wonder if it's the same person we're looking for?"

"Liz, give me a couple of hours and let me find out what happens on the 24th floor", said the editor.

"Do you think it's worth checking out the plumber?", asked Liz tentatively.

"No, my instincts say, this Edward Andrews building person is our guy", the editor said confidently.

After a brief pause, she went on, "Look, I know of an apartment that looks towards that building. I wonder if we can see what's going on from there? I'll call you in a few hours after I set a few things up."

| 41 |

The stakeout

Saturday Night

As Liz and Ray walked to the building, they could hear a band playing somewhere nearby over the hum of air conditioners and city traffic sounds. Someone was belting out some punk rock with a banshee vocal at a reasonable volume. It had energy and anarchy but not much in the way of a tune.

Liz's editor had set up access from this building that looked towards the Edward Andrews and Associates Building.

As per the editor's instructions, they climbed the stairs to the roof to avoid being seen. It didn't take long before they'd begun talking about why elevators were such a good idea and the further they went up, the less conversation there was. It was simply a matter of conserving breath. There were a lot of stairs and they stopped and rested every few flights at the start, then every flight and finally during each flight.

When they reached the top and pushed open the door to the roof they tried to catch their breath while their hearts were still pounding from the exertion of the climb. With the wind whipping through their hair and pulling at their clothing, they walked slowly to the edge of the roof and looked down. It was a long way down to the street. Laughter, music and snippets of conversations merged with general traffic noise floating up from the streets below.

As they oriented themselves, they could see the Blue Sky Tower building in front of them and began working out which floor was the 24th. Liz had her binoculars out and was scanning the building while Ray tried to count floors. It was harder than he'd imagined. He'd some vague recollection that buildings like this didn't have 13th floors. "Is that true", he asked Liz.

"I'm not sure. We should have checked". Liz got out her phone and brought up the building's website.

After a few minutes tapping, she suggested that it must be one of three floors and they trained their binoculars on each floor in turn.

"I reckon it's the bottom one of the three", said Liz.

"I agree", Ray said, "I've been counting down from the top of the building. The top floor is the 51st. Which means in this building there is no 13th floor and the 24th floor is really the 23rd."

"I wonder why they do it?"

Liz said, "According to Google, it's called *'triskaidekaphobia'*. Fear of the number 13. It's still common. The Empire State building, The Eiffel Tower, lots of hospitals. None of them have a 13th floor. All those buildings go from the 12th to the 14th floor."

"Who would have thought that superstition would still be applied today?"

At the mention of superstition, they both started hearing the Stevie Wonder classic in their heads and started nodding and moving their heads in a slow side to side silent dance while mouthing the words *'very superstitious'*.

Ray chuckled. "Do you remember when we first met and I asked you if you were superstitious and you said, No, just normal stitious."

Liz smiled. "Yeh, I was a bit of a smart arse back then."

"I liked it". He reached over and squeezed her hand. She squeezed back.

"Right, can you see anything?" Ray asked.

"Not yet. There doesn't seem to be anyone around on that floor. All the lights are on but I can't see anyone. They all seem to have gone home. I'll set up the camera and then we can have a bite to eat."

Ray lowered his binoculars and looked up at the top of the building. Wow, 51 stories is a long way up. High above the building there seemed to be a bright light.

"Liz, what's that light above the building?"

She looked up from her camera at the light. "I don't know. It doesn't seem to be moving fast enough to be a plane. Could it be a helicopter? No that doesn't seem right either. I s'pose it's a UFO."

"It's not a UFO," Ray dismissed gently.

"How do you know?" demanded Liz.

"Well, I don't know what it is but it still isn't a UFO", Ray said defensively.

"That's exactly what it is until you can identify it", Liz declared, "Then it's an IFO."

"IFO?" Ray sounded puzzled.

"Identified Flying Object. Right now, it is still a UFO... Unidentified."

"Okay, smartass, it's a UFO. You know they call them UAP's now for some reason. Unidentified Aerial Phenomena."

"Yeh, I know," Liz nodded, "What do you think it is?"

"Who knows. It's probably just a slow-moving plane."

They continued to watch the light for another few minutes before they spoke again.

"I still can't work out what it is", Liz said.

"Me neither", Ray added.

"I thought for a while it was a helicopter," Liz mumbled, "but then it seemed to roll over or something. Anyway, I don't think that helicopters can do that."

"It seems to be coming closer", Ray's voice rising in intensity.

"Have you got your camera set up yet Liz? I'll try and get it with my phone but you know how that works out. A shaky, blurry background with some faint light in the distance that when you blow it up, will be so pixelated, it'll look fake, even if it's not."

Liz thought about what was happening. They were getting carried away with the moment. This was supposed to be a stakeout, not an episode of the X-Files.

Ray called, "It's coming this way!"

It was still hard to judge how far away it was and to get some perspective on the size of the object. If it was far away then it was like a big plane and if it was close then it was enormous.

It was too dark with too many distracting lights for the phone to automatically focus and she tried to make adjustments for the dark, zoom in and then focus on the lights. It was all taking time.

The wind was now starting to gust more strongly as the lights became clearer.

"Have you got a shot yet?", Ray yelled.

As Liz finally got the whole shot into view, Ray recognised the shape.

"It's a blimp", he said disappointedly.

"A what?"

"A hot air balloon. An airship!"

"Oh...", the rising hysteria deflating like a lead zeppelin.

They started to laugh. Their built-up emotions over the last few days overflowed and laughter took them over.

"I thought we were going to have a close encounter", Ray said finally, through gasps.

"Me too", Liz agreed. "Wow, it's so easy to get caught up in that stuff."

Ray looked at Liz affectionately. "This is fun. I wouldn't have missed it for the world."

"Me neither. I'm so glad you're here Ray."

"Me too. If you've got your camera recording the 24th floor, I reckon it's time to have our sandwiches and a cup of coffee."

After watching until after midnight, they returned to the ground floor and walked out onto the street and headed for the car.

"Are you ready to head home or do you fancy a quick drink and a bit of music?", asked Liz challengingly. I'm still a bit wired. We passed a jazz bar on the way here. I think it was called *'The Rephrygadorian Mode'*. I know it's not what we usually listen to but it's on the way."

"Did you see who was playing?"

"No."

As they approached the bar, a group of older drunk people staggered out, noisily laughing, invigorated by the night air.

Well there should be room at least. They peered in the window. There were only twenty or thirty people inside, mostly seated at tables, drinking wine. They walked in and looked for a table. The four-piece band was playing something old and soulful.

"Who's the band?", she asked?

"I think it's The Turtlenecks", said Ray, "I don't suppose that's their name but they are fairly old."

They were enchanted by the four musicians enjoying themselves. The band had just started their final set and were playing classics that Ray or Liz vaguely knew from movies and TV. Mostly The Simpsons. They played *'George Gershwin's Summertime'* which they knew from *'The Shawshank Redemption'* and *'The Simpsons'.* Then *'Erroll Garner's Misty'.* Then the Sinatra classic, *'Fly me to the moon'* and finished up with the classic from the movie *'Casablanca - As time goes by'.* Each song reminded them of different Simpsons episodes. It added an extra dimension.

Neither Ray nor Liz knew who wrote the songs before but thankfully, the singer introduced each one fondly as if describing a beloved family member.

It was surprisingly toe-tapping and enjoyable and they stayed for two glasses of red wine each.

| 42 |

Domestic problems

Sunday Morning

Liz woke before the alarm and just lay there running through the previous night in her mind. What does it all mean? She looked over at Ray. He was sleeping on his back, mouth open and making intermittent gurgly, spluttering sorts of noises.

She smiled. She really needed him at the moment. He'd avoided asking the direct question and instead just gone along with what she needed. He still thought that her breakdown was about the death of Angie Murray. She knew she'd share it one day, just not today.

She got up and went into the bathroom and stared at herself in the mirror.

Who is this person looking back at me? Do I know them?

She looked older. The lines around her eyes seemed more accented and showed the signs of strain. She tried to make faces at herself in the mirror. She wasn't sure about this Botox stuff. She mightn't do it again.

Will we ever find out what happened?

Will this be one of those events that never gets explained? The investigation just peters out because there's not enough evidence, not enough interest. The people investigating get moved on to more pressing cases and it all just fades away. This happens far more than people realise, why did she think this would be any different?

On her first investigative journalism project, what was the likelihood that she would get to the bottom of it, publish her critically acclaimed story and win a Walkley award or whatever you get these days.

Ray appeared beside her. "Morning love, how are you?"

"Good, I'm just running it all over in my mind again... and again. It's doing my head in."

"Me too. What's say we make a coffee, sit down and go through it from scratch."

"That sounds like a plan", said Liz thankfully.

Ray made coffee and they sat around the kitchen table.

"Okay, where do you want to start?", asked Liz.

"Let me have a go at putting together what you have so far", said Ray. "A woman was run over and died at the scene. Turned out to be the woman that you'd just started interviewing for work. You spent three hours with her on the day she died.

"Yes, my editor organised it."

"The police don't seem to think that it's suspicious, most likely a hit and run accident and they have now eliminated all except two vehicles. One is a corporate van and the other belongs to a plumber. Both have been reported stolen. Two stolen cars, seems a bit of a coincidence, doesn't it. Plus, both stolen cars seem to have vanished."

"The police have traced one car back to Edward Andrews and Associates which owns a big building in the city centre."

"Somehow, the editor knows someone in the Edward Andrews building was one of Angie's clients."

"Our police friend, Officer Churchward was able to get footage of the building which shows Angie going into the building a few days before she died."

"We now know that she was going to the 24th floor and it's listed as a private floor."

"So we need to find out who's on the 24th floor and what they've got to do with anything."

"Hmmm. Could it just be a coincidence? Who is this Edward Andrews anyway? Is he alive? A real person? Does he work there? We need to find out about him too".

"I suspect that your editor probably knows him, or at least knows of him."

"Okay let's get showered and dressed and go into town and have a closer look at the inside of this building."

Liz went to the bathroom, threw her dressing gown on the side of the bath and started the shower. No water came out. She fiddled with the handles. Nothing. No hot or cold water. Not even a dribble.

"Ray, there's no water", she called out.

Ray was sitting on the toilet, reading the news on his tablet. He got up and flushed. The water gushed into the bowl. It's all normal here, he thought until he realised that the cistern hadn't started to refill. Shit, the water must be out for the whole house.

He went to the bathroom window and looked out into the street. No gushing water geysers that he could see. His French hating neighbour was in his kitchen. Ray called out to him.

"Have you still got running water?"

He nodded vigorously. Ray waved back. "Looks like it's just us."

Liz came in. "It's not just the shower, the basin and the laundry aren't working either."

"Okay, I'll call a plumber", said Ray, as he looked for his phone. "That's strange. Now where did I leave it?"

"Have you seen my phone?"

"Not today."

"That's strange, I would have sworn I left it in the bowl on the bench."

"Maybe it fell out in the car."

"Give it a call."

Liz grabbed her phone and dialled. "It's gone straight to message bank. Maybe it's out of charge."

"I'll go and check the car. Can you call the plumber on your phone?" Ray suddenly realised it was quiet. "Have you seen the pup?"

"I thought you'd let him out."

"No, I thought, you did."

Ray went in search of his phone and the dog.

By lunchtime, they'd not started on the case. Ray was still trying to find his phone, the dog seemed to be missing and organising the plumber was more complicated than they expected. He would get there as soon as he finished the job he was on. Once that was organised, Liz helped Ray look for his phone and the dog. They didn't seem to be anywhere.

It's surprising, thought Liz, Ray is normally so careful with his phone and those sorts of things. She had re-checked the back yard and all the dog's usual hiding places but couldn't find him.

The plumber arrived about one o'clock and got to work straight away. It only took him a few minutes to identify the problem.

"The Water Authority has cut you off. Haven't you paid your bill or something? Everything seems fine inside the house; they just aren't giving you any water."

"Huhh? That doesn't make any sense. Why would that happen?" Ray was confused. "We don't have an outstanding bill, do we?"

"No. Absolutely not", said Liz emphatically. "Well, I don't think so. It should just come out as a regular payment."

"I suggest that you give them a ring", said the plumber.

Ray looked up the number on the website and Liz called it.

After 5 cycles of the ring back tone, the recorded message kicked in. "Your call is important to us, you are 34th in the queue. This is the shortest way to speak to anyone at the Water Authority. Please be patient, we are currently experiencing long delays."

"This is going to take a while", said Liz reluctantly.

The plumber declared that this was outside of his skill set and after checking their contact details, he left 15 minutes later smiling, knowing he was going to be charging an hour's callout fee for 15 minutes work. "Ahhh... life's good", wondering if he should've asked for cash?

It took nearly 25 minutes on the phone to get through to a human at the Water Authority. The wait music was some bland classical music that she didn't recognise.

Liz didn't know a lot about classical music. It all sounded like movie scores to her.

A live human female voice eventually came on and introduced herself as *'Sandy'* and Liz spent a further five minutes establishing that she was who she said she was and she lived where she said she lived, finally getting to explain the situation.

The call centre operator at the other end listened politely, punctuating the conversation with sympathetic "hmmms", "aahs" and "ah huhs". "Well, that sounds terrible", she said, "No showers or flushing toilets today. Let me see what I can find out."

Ray joined Liz in the kitchen, still unable to find his phone. Liz had her phone on speaker and they could hear the operator tapping away on a keyboard. After a few moments, she said, "Well that's odd."

"What's odd?"

"Well, there actually is a disconnect water notice for your house. Are you sure that you didn't request it for some reason, have you just sold the house or bought it?"

"No, we've been here for 15 years. Can you undo it? We do want water please."

"I'll need to check with my supervisor, in case I'm missing some important point, but as far as I can see, an order for disconnecting the water was put into the system yesterday and marked critically urgent. It appears to be related to a health & safety issue raised by city maintenance workers. Please hold on, while I find out some more."

Her voice was replaced with some more classical music that was a bit too loud and was starting to distort on the phone's speakers. Liz reached for the phone and turned down the volume.

"Why do they do that? Don't they know how much it annoys people. Or is it a strategy to make people hang up?"

Ray sighed, "Well, it doesn't sound like it's going to get sorted out before close of business today, does it? What do you want to do? Do you want to check into a hotel until it's fixed? I would love a shower."

They chatted about where they might go until the operator came back replacing the music on the phone. "Are you still there?"

"Yep. Still here."

"I've spoken with my supervisor and we can't really explain it. The health and safety issue doesn't affect your property and so it shouldn't have needed to be touched. We are just looking at where our crews are and when we can get someone to address this. Unfortunately, it looks like it will not be today. We will make every effort to get someone to your place tomorrow, first thing."

"I'll give you my number to call me back in the morning and I'll send you an update via text."

"I am so sorry for the inconvenience", said Sandy and ended the call.

"WTF is going on today", said Liz, "I'm starting to get worried about the pup."

There was a polite knock on the door.

Liz answered it and much to her relief it was Carol from next door holding the pup. "I just found him in my backyard. There must be a hole somewhere."

"Oh, thank God", said Liz the atheist. "I was just saying to Ray that I was really starting to worry. Thank you so much for bringing him over. Is there any news on Eric and Simon?"

Carol suddenly looked very tearful and shaking her head, said "No, nothing yet". "I have no idea what is going on."

"Do you want to come in? For some reason we have no water. I can put together a Gin and tonic pretty quickly or a soft drink."

Carol shook her head. "Thanks, but no thanks. I really don't like to be away from the phone or home very much in case I miss something or someone important. My friend Wendy has been staying with me since they went missing. I'm not sure how I would be coping if she wasn't there. The police seem to have no clue so far."

"It just doesn't make any sense." She then repeated exactly the same phrase. "It just doesn't make any sense. Look Liz, we'll catch up soon, I promise", said Carol as she turned and walked back home.

"Thanks for bringing the dog back. I hope you get some good news soon."

Liz shut the door and leant against the closed door holding the pup tightly. "Whew! What a situation to be in. Her heart went out to Carol. She seemed like such a nice person and they seemed like such a happy family. What on Earth had happened?"

Just then she heard Ray yell loudly from somewhere in the house. "I found it! I found my phone. It was in the laundry basket!"

| 43 |

The hitman gets ready

Sunday Afternoon

The hitman was studying the screens in front of him intently. This was suburbia. One of the hardest places for him to work, especially at weekends.

In cities with lots of people, general indifference and focus on other things, it made it easier to be anonymous. In suburbia, there is usually at least one person that is aware of every person and car that enters the street.

In the old days, it used to be the curtains discreetly moving. Nowadays they all have video phones at their doors and elaborate security systems strategically set up to view the whole street. In his mind, there was always a bunch of nosy grannies glued to their phones watching everything that happened in the street. In this environment, any unrecognised car or person hanging around will be logged and reported to the local neighbourhood watch very quickly.

The other complication seemed to be that the neighbourhood was on high alert because Ray and Liz's neighbour and son had disappeared recently and police were still maintaining a presence in the area. By his reckoning, they were still checking the street every hour or so. The case had been highly publicised and still no one had any idea what had happened. All these things made the house a dangerous place to go but a plan was forming.

He would go in the middle of the night when the street was asleep. In and out between the police's hourly checks in a nondescript car and clothing. Actually, this might be one of those opportunities for one of those high powered electric off road bikes. They were silent, powerful and had a long range. He would be able to go places that few other vehicles could. Yes, this was taking shape. Night vision goggles and an electric bike would make him silent and invisible. Okay, that's a good start. It usually worked. He subconsciously rubbed the scars on his knee from the last time he'd used an electric bike. Those bloody dogs.

Now what about getting away. What route and to where? He pushed back in his chair and looked at the monitors. These had worked out well.

He'd *'borrowed'* a delivery van and used it to place small camera packages around the house and neighbourhood. They were his own design from parts he could get easily and anonymously. The package included 4k video, thermal and infrared imaging, movement detection and audio. It was a powerful combination.

"It'll have to be tonight", he thought decisively. It's 5:00 pm now and it'll be dark soon. Research suggested that most people get up and go to the toilet between 2:00 am to 4:00 am. So, he decided to aim for 1:00 am. He should be in and out in 30 minutes max, so they'll not have much of a chance to accidentally notice him.

He was just about to organise his gear when he noticed Ray and Liz were leaving the house with a suitcase.

???

What's going on now? They hadn't planned to go away. There was nothing in their calendars. He watched them load the car, get in and drive away.

Okay, that changes everything.

He followed their movements through the tracking device he'd placed on the underside of their vehicle.

They drove to a local hotel car park and stopped.

They're staying at a hotel?

!*$#! WTF

Why?

Did they suspect something or is it completely unrelated?

Okay, to deal with them in the hotel could be problematic. Hotels usually had video camera surveillance and reasonably good security. Maybe he could lure them out. He tried to relax and think. Maybe it's time for a disguise.

A new plan started to form. He could create something that forces the evacuation of the whole building, then using a disguise, he could isolate them or move them to a place where there are no cameras or witnesses. Right and then what? They need to be taken out with no sound or trace. That rules out guns, knives and explosives.

He had it. Nice and simple. He would cause the evacuation of the hotel and while they were all outside, he would slip in and place a silent gas cylinder in their room. It would seep out overnight and they would die peacefully in their sleep. The one he liked to use was made to look like a light globe. After it finished releasing the gas, a chemical exothermic reaction fused the insides into a plastic object that could pass very close physical inspection. Before and after, it appeared to be a very normal light globe.

He could use his fireman's supervisor disguise. That would give him the authority to move around freely and a reason to be in any room.

Okay, this is taking shape. He checked the time. 7:04 pm.

The next few hours were spent gathering the equipment he needed and thinking through each step and by 10:30 he was basically ready. He checked the tracking devices and his monitors.

Liz and Ray were still at the hotel and hadn't moved very far in the last hour. They were probably just chilling in their room. All quiet in their home, street and neighbourhood.

He looked up the insignia for the closest fire station. As far as he could see no one had really shiny name badges and equipment. Everything looked a bit used and knocked about. His disguise was too shiny and new looking. He spent 20 minutes ageing his disguise and checking himself in the mirror, looking at his reflection admiringly. Ahh. That's better.

He removed the fireman disguise revealing his basic all black ninja gear.

After a final check of his gear, he drove to the spot he'd selected. His stealth van worked beautifully. No light leakage, no external signs. A very average looking white van. In 15 minutes, he'd placed his devices around the hotel. These were small scale electro-magnetic pulse weapons. He had strategically placed them to take out crucial monitoring systems. The camera system, lighting and environment. He'd placed a larger EMP device at the electrical substation and one at the external transformer vault which was delightfully old and susceptible to EMP. After he entered the building, he'd also place one at the internal power distribution panel.

Finally, he targeted two fire sensors that would trigger the alarm and evacuation. One on the roof and one near the lobby. From his van he could target microwave devices at both of the sensors. They would heat up slowly, move out of their safe ranges and trigger.

Once they'd been triggered, alarms would go off, the fire brigade would be called automatically and the building evacuated. Once the building was evacuated, the electro-mag pulse devices he'd placed would go off taking out power to the whole building including all the cameras, lights and communications. He'd then join the fire brigade as they sweep the building. He just needed to get to Ray and Liz's room, change the light bulb and get out.

The fire brigade would find nothing and everyone would eventually be let back in. Ray and Liz would return to their room, go to sleep and when the movement sensor recognised they had stopped moving, wait 45 minutes and then release the gas causing them to die a painless and peaceful death. That would finally bring this whole horrible saga to an end. What a mess. All this trouble because of one woman's reflexes.

His client wasn't happy and wondered if he'd try and kill him too. All because the hit attracted attention. He knew it wasn't his best work. That unlucky thing again.

In his line of work, it was better to be completely average. To arouse no suspicion at all. His execution of the job had created sympathy for the woman that probably wouldn't have happened if she hadn't been young and attractive. Also, the nature of her death made some people squeamish... it might have been different if they knew how she made a living. Lawyer and sex worker. Neither profession was held in particularly high regard by the general public.

The bit that upset his client and everyone who knew the details was the fact that it had taken two goes to kill her. The first hit hadn't been enough and he'd backed up and made sure. That's the bit that had people up in arms. It was a stupid, stupid thing to do and he'd been regretting it on an hourly basis ever since.

He checked the temperature of the fire sensors. It looked like the one on the roof would go first so he turned the microwave transmitter down slightly. Ideally, he wanted the two alarms to go off within a minute or so of each other. Fifteen minutes later, he could see that they were about to trigger. He continued getting into his fire supervisor disguise. As he was putting on his boots, he heard the fire alarm go off.

11:54pm

That's good, most of them will already be in bed.

Within eight minutes, the fire brigade arrived and a trail of people were being evacuated and escorted from the hotel. He could see a hundred or so people gathering in an evacuation zone and hotel staff with clipboards and tablets running around, trying to organise and calm the disgruntled mob. The staff could probably do with a sheep dog or two, he thought chuckling.

At this point the first of the electro-mag pulse devices went off with a loud bang and flash of light as the hotel was plunged into darkness. The crowd noises increased as people tried to take in what had just happened. The fire truck lights seemed to become brighter somehow and small pockets of light appeared around the carpark as phone lights were brought out.

He checked himself in the mirror. A fireman supervisor looked back. Completely convincing. Giving himself a confident smile in the mirror, he slipped out to join the confusion.

He wasn't challenged as he entered the rear of the building and made his way to the reception area, picked up a master key and placed an EMP device near the internal power distribution panel. Moving quickly up the stairs, he made his way to the floor where Ray and Liz were staying.

Looking up and down the corridor, all seemed clear. He couldn't hear anything unusual and his night vision goggles made everything appear the usual nightmarish, eerie green world.

He made his way to their room using the master key that he'd grabbed on the way and was in and out of the room in 30 seconds.

The bulb replaced; he headed back up the corridor. Suddenly, he could hear voices in front of him. At least two people.

They were in the stairwell.

He listened carefully.

They were moving floor to floor working their way from the roof down.

They must have gone to check the roof sensor.

He retraced his steps and went back into Ray and Liz's room. It was probably safer here, now this floor had been cleared.

He just needed to get out before the power was restored or he would be highly visible. He walked to the window and looked out at the chaos below. The flashing lights somehow made the darkness darker. He looked up. No moon and a fair bit of cloud. Perfect weather for this sort of job.

As he watched the people running around like a disturbed ant's colony, he smiled and thought, I created this. They are all reacting to something I made happen. He took in a deep satisfying breath as he enjoyed the power of it. The power to change people's lives. Another couple of minutes and he'd descend another few floors. Check out the situation, descend the final floors and walk out either the lobby or the rear exit.

He waited a couple of minutes and then made his move. Both the lobby and the rear exit seemed busy.

He considered his options. I need a distraction to make this happen.

Flicking a small switch in his pocket, a special device in the van started to charge. Another device of his own making. When it was fully charged it would send a very unique series of high intensity low frequency sounds which made a lot of the car alarms in the carpark go off by shaking their impact vibration sensors. It was a combination Sonic Boom Generator operating in the 2Hz to 8Hz range coupled with a high frequency whistle in the 2KHz to 8KHz range.

With a BOOM, the device triggered dozens of car alarms. It was a crazy, discordant sound that made him pleased he had his earpieces.

Moving slowly and deliberately he joined the group of people going to investigate. He'd shouted, "Is it an earthquake?" before joining the larger group, which had the required effect, adding a bit more drama.

During this confusion, he just moved with the crowd which was mostly made up of confused hotel guests with a few fire, police and hotel staff trying to maintain a sense of order. It was dark enough and there was enough angst in the group to keep everyone focussed on other things.

He separated from the group and circled back to his van. Inside, he quickly changed his clothes, stashing them in one of the secret storage lockers in the front of the van. He then just watched what was happening around him.

Happy with the chaos he'd created, he watched and waited a few minutes then slipped the van into gear and slowly drove away.

| 44 |

Fire

Late Sunday Evening

Liz and Ray were rudely awakened from a deep sleep when the fire alarm in the hotel went off.

As they tried to work out what was happening, they could hear someone coming up the corridor, knocking on doors, saying, "Fire alarm, you must evacuate the building."

They gathered dressing gowns around them and heading out of the room, grabbing their swipe cards, phones and wallets before joining the others in the corridor.

"Remember to take your swipe cards", yelled a staff member.

Other guests were appearing in the hall in various states of undress and night clothing. It was obvious that most people had been in bed, but some were still dressed in their evening finery. A few were standing around waiting for the elevator.

"The elevators won't work in a fire. They aren't safe", declared a staff member trying hard not to sound patronising, "You'll have to walk down the stairs. Please follow me."

The staff member began guiding the group to the stairs and a low murmur filled the stairwell, which was amplified and reverberated by the bare concrete walls.

Everyone seemed to be confident that it was a false alarm or a drill and no one seemed to be panicking. That was until an elderly woman tripped and fell into the people in front of her. The murmur volume increased as this stopped the flow of people moving down the stairs. The one's in front were trying to tell the people above, '*Hold up*' a woman has fallen.

There was a tangible increase in tension in the stairwell as those above that couldn't see what was happening were becoming tense. The orderly evacuation had just become disorderly.

Liz and Ray talked about the moment afterwards. "Did you feel the group panic?"

They could feel the group start to panic as the idea that they could be stuck in the stairwell, threatening their personal survival, was about to turn this nice orderly evacuation into a free for all. It was close. They both felt the panic rise in them and those around them before someone wiser started to shout out progress reports.

The confident strong voice averted a very serious situation. Who knows how it might have played out otherwise. Anyway, it was enough to snap the crowd back into a cohesive group but it did highlight to them both how close anarchy can be when individual survival is challenged.

What was that one? Something about people are great individually but a group or mob is another beast entirely.

Once they were outside, Liz turned to Ray, "I don't think I can handle this. I just want to go to sleep. Do you want to just go back home? It looks like it will be a while before this lot quietens down. We could be home in 20 minutes and in bed in 30."

"That sounds much better. I do prefer our own bed."

"We'll come back tomorrow and get our stuff."

They looked around the crowded car park area. To Ray, it looked like an Arthur Dent and Hugh Hefner convention, with a few Agnes Browns thrown in. Ray usually went to bed each night dressed as Arthur Dent.... if it was good enough for Arthur Dent to go from one end of time and the universe it should be okay for round the house. It also worked really well as a last-minute New Year's Eve costume.

As a costume it's just pyjamas, slippers and a dressing gown. If you don't specify a type for each it's nearly Hugh Hefner. To do Hugh, you need fancier pyjamas, maybe silk or something shiny or slippery, slippers and a robe that looks a bit like a smoking jacket. Hugh was also a bit more nautical. A sea captain's hat completed the look. Arthur is more basic flannel pyjamas, plain slippers and plain dressing gown.

Over the years Ray alternated between the two looks. Hugh and Arthur. Since the pandemic and now that he was working a lot more from home, the *'Hugh'* look even worked okay on video calls.

"Hey Liz, can you take a photo of this scene? My phone is still on the charger in the room. This is the weirdest thing that's happened in a while." Liz dug her phone out of her dressing gown and took a few shots. She checked. The photos didn't really capture it.

Just then there was a big bang and a bright flash of light and then it went dark. All the lights in the car park went out. They held hands instinctively, Liz fumbling with her phone to turn on the torch. It was confusing in the dark, with all the flashing lights and car alarms blaring. Using the torch to find their way they headed off in search of their car. In a few minutes they'd found their car and spent the next few minutes rubbing their hands together vigorously to get warm as they waited for the car heater to thaw them out.

Outside the car was a mixture of flashing police and fire engine lights with the odd car alarm. The lights were having a strobe effect and made the people move in slow motion. It was like watching a zombie movie. It could have been a scene from Shaun of the Dead.

| 45 |

On the move

Early Monday Morning

He couldn't believe it. They were on the move again. It looked like they were going back home. All that effort wasted. I am so unlucky. Again! Why do my plans never work out? He took a slow deep breath through his nose and exhaled slowly though his mouth. Hmmm. Back to plan A. He still had the bike and the other equipment. Could he use the same trick? The light globe?

He'd already checked out their home security system. No problem there. He followed them home and watched them go inside. Through the window he could see that they were seated at the kitchen table having a final cuppa before bed.

He athletically scaled the house and slipped in the upstairs window. He took some equipment from his backpack and fed the knockout gas into the kitchen below. Within five minutes he heard two heads hit the table.

He came downstairs quickly and looked at the two sleeping figures. Actually, I wouldn't mind a cup of tea myself while I'm waiting, he thought. They're not going anywhere now and I want to take my time.

He'd always had a cruel streak. His parents and teachers had noticed. Not liking cats was one sign and being cruel to insects and other animals was another. It seems that the reason psychopaths don't like cats is that cats won't recognise you as superior. They're not eager to please.

Everything they do is important for them and psychopaths just can't stand it. That helio-centric problem again. The world should revolve around them.

He really wanted to hurt Ray and Liz for the trouble they'd put him through. The fact that they had no idea about any of this, didn't really come into the picture. He checked his watch. Probably another forty minutes or so before they woke up.

He looked around the kitchen. All sorts of knives. He would really like to make them understand that they'd cost him dearly and they should pay. He fought hard to overcome the urge as his original plan was to make it look like a gas leak in the kitchen. He went to fill the kettle. No water came out. Why have they got no water?

He started to remove items from his backpack and place them on the table when he felt strong arms brush past him and in one impossibly quick move, cable tied his arms and feet together.

"Wha...?"

Tape was placed over his mouth and something placed over his eyes. In less than 2 seconds he was completely helpless.

"Take him", ordered Seth Barlow.

A couple of darkly clad figures efficiently picked him up and took him from the room.

Seth Barlow looked at Ray. He could still see his childhood neighbour. The little kid was still in there somewhere. He was tempted to wait and talk to him but he knew he couldn't. Their lives had gone in such completely different directions and they couldn't be brought back together. It made him feel good to do this. He'd saved his only friend from childhood and he'd never know.

What with doing this good deed and removing a few prolific litterers, maybe he was changing. He wasn't going to fight it or over analyse it.

It'd been good for him to see Ray's life. It was so normal. It had ups and downs and highs and lows. He'd found a good partner. Liz had her own problems and history but she seemed to be a good person and they appeared to love each other. If things had gone differently, maybe he could've had a life like this. Hard to imagine now.

Seth Barlow knew that the one that asked him to clean up this situation would take care of the unlucky hitman. The guy just did not seem to be cut out for this type of work. He seemed to be exceptionally unlucky.

He instructed his team to carry Ray and Liz upstairs and put them to bed. They were already dressed for it. They were also given a shot to counteract the effect of the gas, so that they would wake up feeling good.

What was that stuff called again? "Happy Juice?"

He gave out his final instructions to the team and they all quietly left before the next police car passed along the street, completely unaware that they'd missed everything.

Seth had read about Ray and Liz's neighbour and kid going missing. He thought, if the unlucky hitman had succeeded tonight, this would have become an infamous street.

| 46 |

Disposing of the Hitman

Early Monday Morning

The hitman awoke to a continuous droning sound that he couldn't quite place. It wasn't a lawn mower; it wasn't a train or truck. Whatever it was he wished it would shut up and let him get back to sleep. He moved to sit up. A sharp pain shot up both arms and he didn't actually move at all.

"What the...?"

He slowly realised that he was actually tied up and probably in the boot of a car. That was the sound he couldn't place.

"Why on earth was he here?"

Who'd he pissed off lately. Or ever for that matter. Enough to want to tie him up and put him in the boot of a car. Was this Edward Andrews cleaning up the situation?

He was able to ponder this for another hour before the car finally slowed down and made its way slowly over a bumpy gravel road and then stopped.

The voices got clearer as car doors opened and slammed shut. Straining to hear any of the conversation, he couldn't quite make it out. There were 2 voices but he'd heard three car doors. The murmuring stopped and he realised that he couldn't hear any other noises. It was nearly silent. Where can you go that is nearly silent, he wondered? His pulse rate, which was already racing, suddenly got a second wind and tried to double itself as he heard the key fob beep and the boot clicked and opened.

For some reason he'd expected bright sunlight when the boot opened but it was just as dark outside as it was inside. There were three faces peering in, eerily lit by a small red glow.

One of them said to the others, "Get him out". They roughly manhandled him out and dumped on the ground that was as hard as cement. Actually, it was cement. As his eyes started to adjust, he realised that he was in a garage or something like it. That can't be good. No one can see or hear me.

As he lay on the cement behind the car wondering and waiting, something unexpected happened. His mobile phone went off. This caused a stir amongst the three men. One of them tried to roll him over and search for the phone. As they were roughly patting his body, he noticed that his arms and legs were suddenly free.

He was free. It was just dumb luck but sometimes dumb luck can be good. Sometimes it's the only luck you've got. He was up quickly and dodging reaching arms when he spotted the open garage door, headed for it and ran and ran and ran.

After a while he began to consider that he should pick a direction. He must have run over a kilometre before he remembered that he wasn't a runner. At the realisation, his heart and lungs decided that they'd been operating under false pretences and refused to cooperate further until a rest period was taken. His knees collapsed underneath him as he nose-dived into the ground.

As he lay on the ground, gasping for breath, his pulse roaring in his ears, he heard the car and saw the lights dance around the trees and sky. He attempted to negotiate a return-to-work agreement with his heart and lungs. They were as sympathetic as a union representative listening to management's reasons for not giving them a 3% pay increase while they all took six figure bonuses.

With much grizzling and groaning he stood up and swayed uncertainly while he gathered his bearings. I could think much clearer if the brass band in my head would just take a few minutes break... The blood pumping in his ears was so loud. The adrenaline, lactic acid build up, hyperventilation and rapid heart rate were a consequence of his fight or flight reflex choosing flight.

He didn't remember being involved in the discussion.

He'd used up a lot of his energy reserves and was starting to feel light-headed, his glycogen stores depleted.

He looked up at the star filled sky. The song was right. They do look like little diamonds in the sky. So beautiful. A star-studded tapestry stretched across the sky. This brief reverie was interrupted by car headlights flashing like a poorly funded underage disco from his youth. Only one light and trying to go in every direction at once.

To run or not to run, that was the question. He decided it was nobler to fall back down and hug the ground as if his life depended on it. Which he was sure it did.

The car slowed down but kept going as they searched for him. He lay there gasping for breath as quietly as he could. I must get fitter. I must get fitter. If I live through this, I will go back to the gym every day.

I promise. Oh God, do I promise.

Who am I kidding?

I think it is time to change careers.

It's okay God, I get the message. Message received loud and clear! I'm not cut out for this sort of work.

After walking and stumbling for several miles he found a deserted highway and was trying to work out where he was, when he saw a vehicle approaching in the distance. The headlights seemed incredibly bright in the darkness and the blinding light grew larger and more dazzling which made it hard and then impossible to see the ground in front of him causing him to lurch, fall and stumble onto the road, striking his head and shoulder on the hard road surface.

The last thing that passed through his mind before the truck hit him was, "Why did I bother giving up smoking?"

| 47 |

The truck driver

Monday Morning

Seth Barlow felt the truck bounce as it ran over the unlucky hitman. Karma is a bitch he thought.

Simon had done it again.

His instructions had been simple. Pick up this fuel truck and drive a very specific route leaving at precisely 4:07 am while maintaining a constant speed. Under no circumstances was he to deviate from the route or speed. He must also stay in his lane, no matter what. No swerving to avoid animals on the road or any other obstacle. By 4:43am, he would understand what his task was about. He looked at the clock on the dashboard. 4:44.

He was to continue to an abandoned mine where he was to drive the truck into an old mineshaft, after rigging a low-tech fuse which would ignite the truck, destroying it and causing the shaft to collapse on top of it, covering it forever.

He'd no idea that this job was related to the unlucky hitman. He'd just received instructions from Simon and after seeing the impossible so many times now, he just trusted there was a good reason. He had no idea how Simon could possibly know the things that he did... but somehow, he did.

As he watched the truck disappear down the mine shaft, he waited expectantly for the explosion. The ground around him shook violently like an earthquake as the mineshaft filled itself in and completely covered the truck.

Walking back up the track to the vehicle that should be waiting for him, he wondered idly, "What's the bet Simon owns this old mine?" ...and then... "I wonder whether Edward Andrews will make old bones?"

| 48 |

The final chapter

Tuesday Morning

Someone was knocking on the door like a demented percussionist. Ray went to answer it. Carefully looking through the door viewer, he said "Your boss is here".

"O'shit." said Liz.

"I didn't know she was Irish?", Ray tried to make a joke.

"Give me a tick, stall her, stall her", shouted Liz.

"I can hear you both from the porch, if that helps", chimed in the editor.

Ray opened the door and a long flowing assortment of complementary colours breezed into the centre of the room.

Looking from one to the other she said, "How are you both?"

Before either had a chance to answer, she continued with "I have important news."

She held up the front page of the paper. Under the heading 'Highflyer arrested' was a picture of Officer Sally Churchward arresting Edward Andrews flanked by Captain Egan.

She read from the article out loud. "Edward Andrews was arrested this morning for a range of charges including fraud and financial irregularities. It is believed that he ran several high-class brothels and escort services amongst his legitimate businesses. Further charges are expected to be laid in the coming weeks. Federal officers are now investigating and several high value assets have been seized.

"Apparently, when he was arrested, he was livid", the editor smirked with satisfaction.

"So, there was no grand conspiracy, Angie had simply become a nuisance, then a pain in the arse who had to be dealt with. She'd worked out that Edward Andrews was actually her boss and ran all sorts of sex worker services around the city and liked things as they were. Trying to organise an alliance or union and advocating for sex workers rights was emboldening and empowering the people that were working for him. He didn't like it."

"He believed that to maintain leadership you must make examples of people every now and then and so he decided to make an example of Angie to control the rest. To him it was simply business. She was making business more difficult. Her mistake was telling him about it. If she'd just done it, he would have been caught off guard. It might have made a difference. Maybe it was inevitable once she'd chosen that path."

Neither Ray or Liz had spoken yet.

She stared at them expectantly. "Well?"

"Good," said Ray and Liz at the same time.

The editor didn't seem satisfied with that response. "You have both done really well. I'm impressed... but it's over now. We know what happened. It's time to stop your investigation and move on to something new."

Liz and Ray looked at each other sceptically.

The editor charged on. "Now, various pieces of information have come to light during your investigation that really don't need to have any more light shone upon them. I'm sure that I can rely on your sense of honour and discretion."

Liz and Ray both had a "light bulb" moment. They looked at each other knowingly.

Liz looked at the editor squarely and said, "What you mean is that "*you*" were on that list too. You were seeing Angie as a client as well. That's how you were able to set up my interview with her and why the interview was specifically for three hours. You paid her for it. You have been pulling and pushing us all the way through this investigation."

"Yes, all that stuff", said the editor dismissively.

Ray couldn't help himself and asked, "Were you in love with her?"

The editor looked at Ray and then Liz, measuring them up.

"Probably. If you think you were shattered by her death Liz, I was too.

She told me during some pillow talk, that something was up, something big. It involved her boss; her industry and she was very worried that people would either be hurt or go missing.

My editor's nose twitched at the information and thought it could be worth exploring.

I wasn't expecting things to happen so fast but once Angie was killed, I wanted justice for her. That's when I got you involved, Liz. The list didn't come from a friend of Angie's, I made that up. She'd given it to me as security and insurance. Thank God she did or we would never have found the bastard."

"Do you think Edward Andrews will go to prison or will someone '*get*' him?", Liz asked.

My insiders in the police force are telling me that there was a major financial collapse in his legitimate business affairs the previous day. I don't know if it was someone else on the list or someone else entirely but I am truly grateful to them for nailing the slimeball."

Ray and Liz looked at each other, silently acknowledging this woman's questionable lack of sanity and morality. This crazy, ruthless woman had no heart, soul or moral compass. Whether you believed in hell or not, this manipulative woman probably deserved to go there.

"Now Liz, I want you to write up this story keeping some of the more sensitive aspects to ourselves. What do you reckon?"

Liz fell silent for a moment and said, "Okay, on one condition."

"Hmmm, what's that?", asked the editor cautiously.

"Our next-door neighbours, Eric Carver and his son Simon have gone missing. Carol is really distressed. Perhaps I could look into what happened to them?"

| 49 |

The BBQ

Loose ends

Ray was standing at the gas BBQ poking at the sausages, burgers and kebabs as Gabe looked on, dodging plumes of smoke and lapping up the smell of grilling meat.

It was a beautiful day and the backyard was looking great. Liz's fascination with aromatic plants made the backyard a wonderful sensory experience.

Wafts of lavender, jasmine and roses mixed easily with sunscreen, insect repellent and grilling meat.

At the table under the shade sat their neighbour Carol, her friend Wendy, Liz and Officer Sally. They had moved from wine to G & Ts already and were deep in conversation, erupting in rowdy laughter periodically.

"New T-shirt?" asked Gabe, reading the motto, *'I'm in favour of anarchy as long as it's properly organised',* I like it."

So how are things going with Liz? Gabe asked.

"Better", said Ray, "There's still something she won't talk about."

"Apart from all the trauma of it, this has been the best thing we've done for ages. It felt like we're a couple again. Both on the same team, working together. I want to do more of it. It's good for us both to see the other in a constructive way."

"These sausages and burgers are nearly ready."

Ray called out to the group at the table. "Are you ready for food? Are you hungry?"

A chorus of yums ran round the table.

Gabe helped Ray transfer the food from the BBQ plate to serving trays and placed them on the table amongst the salads and condiments.

As they all sat down, Ray said, before we eat, I'd just like to thank you all for coming and I'd like to propose a toast.

To Carol, I hope you can feel our collective love and support.

To Wendy. Carol's wonderful friend. What a legend.

To Officer Sally, a new friend and a guiding light during our recent challenges.

To Gabe and Molly, cherished friends. Thank you for everything.

And finally, to the lovely Liz. I'm so glad you're my wife.

Ray looked around the table, held his glass high and said, "May our glasses be full, our troubles be few, and our friendships strong. Here's to us—today, tomorrow, and always. Cheers!"

There followed a clink of glasses and choruses of "Cheers", one "Salut" and a "Kanpai!".

As they began eating, Wendy asked Sally, "This job of yours must be a challenge. This whole thing with Liz seems like something out of a novel. How on Earth do you turn off from that sort of thing?"

Sally said, "Sorry Wendy. You just reminded me. Liz, I meant to tell you, as a matter of course Angie's DNA was added to the NCIDD. The national DNA database and we got an unexpected match. It seems highly likely that we know who Angie's mother was. She was already in the database", clearly demonstrating that she had not yet learnt to turn off from that sort of thing.

"Unfortunately, her mother died 25 years ago in very sad circumstances. Wrong place at the wrong time. That's why she was listed in the National Criminal Investigation DNA Database. I just thought you'd like to know. It is so sad. Neither of them got past 30."

Liz said, "That is sad."

They all agreed. It was sad.

Officer Sally nodded. The other strange thing that's come to light is that a young couple died in the hotel that Liz and Ray stayed at when their water got cut off. It's unexplained so far and they died the night after you two stayed there. The spooky bit is that they stayed in the same room as you did.

"Wow, that is spooky."

They all agreed. It was spooky.

Liz looked at Carol's glazed unfocussed expression and tried to move the conversation in a new direction. "Anyone got some lighter news? What's new with you Molly?"

"Well, Gabe and I are thinking about our next holiday and maybe starting a new business. We've been doing the same thing for 7 years now and it feels like time for a change."

They chatted as they ate, trying to keep the conversation light.

Carol finished first, excused herself and went indoors to use the bathroom.

Once she was out of earshot, Molly turned to Wendy and said, "I really don't know what to say to Carol. It must be awful. I don't know whether to say anything or not. Have there been any developments or would you rather not talk about it now."

Wendy said, “It’s been hard. There’s no doubt. I’m glad you invited us as Carol is barely keeping it together and this is a welcome diversion.”

“We can talk about it when she gets back if you like. It’s not that she doesn’t want to talk about it, there’s just nothing much to say. Nobody knows anything. The police can’t find a trace of them. No signs of foul play. No messages. Eric is not accessing any bank accounts or making contact with friends or colleagues. It is a complete mystery.”

“Please don’t feel that you have to avoid the topic. It’s central to her every waking thought and she really wants to know. It is hard to overplay the amount of anguish in this. It’s now over a month and we still have no idea what happened.”

“I know that she’s grateful to you both for your support”, looking at Ray and Liz.

“Sometimes I forget for a while and I see it in her too. Some daily task or routine puts Carol in normal mode and then something happens or a thought pops in and then she is straight back to that cloud of disbelief.”

Carol returned to the table.

Wendy said, “I was just explaining that you’re okay talking about what’s going on, just that there’s not that much to say. We don’t know anything. The number of times we’ve wished we had a time machine so that we could go back and see what happened.”

Carol agreed. “To be honest this has been the craziest roller coaster ride of my life. Each day I ride the roller coaster. Up and down. Up and down. High to low.”

“It plays with your head. In the first weeks, every time the phone rang, I was on high alert. Was this the call I’d been waiting for? Now when the phone rings it's more a mixture of trepidation and dread. I can go into high expectations and then crash into another soul crushing because of a lack of information.”

They all looked at Carol. It was a horrible situation to be in. They all felt her pain and anguish.

"You know Carol, we'll help in any way we can", said Liz reaching across to touch her hand.

"I know and I appreciate what you've done already", Carol said, patting Liz's hand.

"I have been off work since it happened and I'll run out of annual leave and long service leave eventually. I'm going to have to make a decision in the next month or so, what I'm going to do."

"This is a welcome distraction as it keeps me away from dark thoughts. I don't want to think the worst."

There was a long pause as everyone digested the situation.

"Enough of that for now", said Carol, "aren't you going to get the instruments out?"

Ray looked at Gabe. "What do ya reckon?"

"I bags the acoustic bass", said Gabe.

"Well, I'll take the acoustic guitar", said Ray.

"I'll get the Congas", said Liz." Do you play anything Wendy? Sally?"

"Maybe later", said Wendy, happy to see what unfolded.

"A definite no for me", said Sally laughing. "No one has ever accused me of being musical."

"What do you play Wendy?", asked Gabe?

"Mostly classical and Jazz", she replied, "but I do know some contemporary stuff."

"She's got a really nice voice", said Carol, "We used to sing and do some harmony bits at uni."

The next hour turned into a jam session and singalong covering a lot of old classics, lightening the mood and lifting their spirits considerably. Molly had such a good voice and moved easily from soulful ballads to belting out rock 'n' roll. Wendy and Carol did some great harmonies and the rhythm section of Ray, Gabe and

Liz were playing songs they'd played for years. Sally seemed happy to join in on the songs she knew and play the plastic egg if she didn't.

Every now and then Liz noticed Carol would vague over and then return to participation. Until there was some resolution for her, this was going to be her life. Trying to fit in with day to day living while dealing with powerful thoughts and feelings that were always threatening to overwhelm her.

Liz wished she could help in some way.

She thought things would be so much easier if this was just a story and she could make a wish.

She thought if I had a wish... I'd wish that they all lived happily ever after.

THE END

| 50 |

Postscript

Back to work

First day back at work after their adventures, Ray boarded his second flight for the day, found his seat and looked carefully to see who his neighbours were. They seemed okay. They didn't appear to be nutters.

The person on his right was reading a physical book called *'Problems with common wisdom'.*

Okay, he hadn't seen that before.

The reader looked up and their eyes met. They did that half smile, half grimace thing people do to acknowledge each other.

He had to ask. "That's a great book title. Is it what it seems?"

"Yeh", said the man engagingly, "it's quite fascinating. Those things that we learn and just take for granted without thinking."

"Like what?"

"Don't put your eggs in one basket."

"Seems wise and sage and all those other things but you can pose some questions."

"Where should you put your eggs?"

"What if you don't have a basket?"

"What if you don't have more than one basket?"

"In fact, there are many circumstances in which it is entirely prudent to put your eggs in one basket. Does this mean that the saying has no value? Is it just the nature of metaphors, that they only apply in certain situations."

"Ooh I like that."

"I must get myself a copy. I love this stuff."

"There's heaps of them. A stitch in time saves nine. Are there times when a stitch in time only saves eight?"

"Good question."

They chatted away amicably for the rest of the flight as they flew off into the sunset.

CHAPTER NOTES

Chapter 2: Friday Phone call

Nocebo: a detrimental effect on health produced by psychological or psychosomatic factors such as negative expectations of treatment or prognosis.

Chapter 3: Cleaning out the spare room

Anagnorisis: Look it up if you need a clue. Examples include a play by Sophocles (circa 500 BC-400 BC) called "Oedipus Rex", the 1999 movie "Sixth Sense" or Darth Vader revealing that he is Luke's father in Star Wars: Episode V – The Empire Strikes Back (1980).

Majestic Fanfare: Orchestral Piece written by British composer Charles Williams in 1935 and introduced to the ABC in the 1950's.

The meek will inherit the earth: Matthew 5:5. Blessed are the meek for they shall inherit the earth.

Agincourt: The Battle of Agincourt was an English victory in the Hundred Years' War in October 1415 near Agincourt, in northern France.

Chapter 4: Give a dog a bad name

Out damn Spot: William Shakespeare, Macbeth, Act II, Scene 2, Line 58.

Macbeth: Probably written 1606-1607 - First performed publicly at the Globe Theatre in London 1611.

Double, double, toil and trouble. Fire burn and cauldron bubble: William Shakespeare, Macbeth, Act IV, Scene 1, Line 10

Chapter 5: Edward Andrews

Haute = High. Couture = Fashion. Coiffure = Hair style. Joaillerie = Jewellery. Parfumerie de niche = Luxury, exclusive perfumes. Horlogerie = Fine watchmaking.

57 facets: The 57 facets in a diamond represent a precise scientific calculation to capture and manipulate light in a way that creates the most dazzling and fiery display possible.

Carat, cut, clarity and colour: The four C's - The factors that determine the value and quality of a diamond.

Chapter 8: On the train

Ray's first and only book: The Art and Optimism of Cord Wiggling.

Chapter 9: Liz's new assignment

Ig Nobel awards: A parody of the Nobel Prizes, the Ig Nobel Prizes are awarded each year around the time the recipients of the genuine Nobel Prizes are announced. It celebrates achievements that "first make people laugh, and then make them think". Created in 1991 by Marc Abrahams.

Darwin awards: The Darwin Awards are a tongue-in-cheek honour started around 1985. It recognizes individuals who have contributed to human evolution by selecting themselves out of the gene pool by either dying or becoming sterilised from their own actions.

Chapter 10: On the plane

The story of the biblical Isaac and his father Abraham: Book of Genesis. Genesis Chapter 22

Five foot twelve: Five foot 12 is the same as 6 feet.

Stockholm Syndrome: Feelings of trust or affection felt in many cases of kidnapping or hostage-taking by a victim towards their captor.

Did they know it's Christmas: Reference to the Band Aid song "Do they know it's Christmas". It was a charity song written in 1984 by Bob Geldof and Midge Ure to raise money for the 1983–1985 famine in Ethiopia.

Harry kills Voldemort in the end: Spoiler

Chapter 11: Angie's request

Geisha Coffee: Originating from the Gori Gesha forest in Ethiopia, Geisha coffee has become a prized possession among coffee aficionados and is considered one of the world's most prestigious and expensive coffees. Geisha coffee is characterised by its delicate floral and sweet notes, often described as having hints of jasmine, chocolate, honey, and even black tea.

Eames lounge with ottoman: The Eames Lounge Chair and Ottoman is one of the most iconic and expensive chairs in the world. Designed by Charles and Ray Eames in 1956 and known for its sleek, modern design and comfortable seating. A new Eames Lounge Chair and Ottoman can cost upwards of $5,000.

Kenneth Williams: Born in 1926, was celebrated for his high-pitched voice, camp mannerisms, and impeccable comedic timing. His most notable work came from his appearances in the *Carry On* film series, where he played memorable roles in 26 of the 31 films. Despite his professional success, Williams battled with depression and alcoholism throughout his life, further exacerbated by his social anxiety and reclusive lifestyle. On April 15, 1988, at the age of 62, Williams passed away from an overdose of barbiturates.

SIM card: SIM card, or Subscriber Identity Module: A small integrated circuit card that's inserted into a mobile phone to store and transmit information to the network. It serves as a subscriber's identification and authentication document, enabling access to cellular services such as making calls, sending and receiving messages, and connecting to the internet.

Signal: Signal is a free and open-source messaging app that uses end-to-end encryption to protect its messages. Only the sender and recipient can read the content of the communications. Signal does not store any data on its servers or share data with third parties. Other features include Ephemeral messaging and Self-destructing photos and videos.

VPN: A virtual private network (VPN) is a secure network that creates a tunnel between your device and a VPN server, encrypting all of your online traffic. This means that your internet service provider (ISP), government agencies, and other third parties can't track your online activity or see the data you are sending and receiving.

Chapter 12: Liz's Story

Alice's Adventures in Wonderland: 1865 novel by Charles Dodgson under the pen name Lewis Carroll.

The role of the Gin and Tonic in the history of the British Empire: In the 18th century, British officers in India and other tropical areas drank gin and tonic. They were trying to fight off malaria which killed thousands of people. The approach during that era was to use quinine powder, which is made from the bark of the cinchona tree to prevent the disease. It does appear to have been effective, but it tasted awful... hence the gin.

Chapter 14: Liz Does Some Research

What a sex worker can teach us about human connection: TEDx Salt Lake City by Nicole Emma.

www.ted.com/talks/nicole_emma_what_a_sex_worker_can_teach_us_about_human_connection?subtitle=en

Chapter 15: Ray's Story

Am-dram: Amateur Dramatics

Borg: Star Trek Voyager reference. Based on the Borg (short for Cyborg) character Seven of Nine (7 of 9).

Oopart: Out of place artifact

Schadenfreude: A German word used to describe the pleasure derived by another person's misfortune.

Dr Strange: Marvel character created by Steve Ditko and first appeared in "Strange Tales #110" in 1963.

The modern scientific method: Cartesian doubt is a systematic process of being sceptical about (or doubting) the truth of one's beliefs. Descartes suggested that because the senses sometimes deceive, we have reason not to trust them.

Hold their breath for long periods: Tom Cruise on the Graham Norton Show cited an example when learning to hold his breath for 4-6 minutes and having to overcome the natural impulse to breathe and also having to remember to start again.

Chapter 16: In the Foyer

Garfield: A comic strip created by Jim Davis in 1978. At one stage it was in the Guinness Book of Records as the most widely syndicated comic in the world.

Chapter 17: The Next Friday Phone call

Reversibility and irreversibility: Concepts in thermodynamics

Chapter 19: Back home

Greenland: A Danish colony until 1953, when it was redefined as a district of Denmark.

John Lloyd: Creator of the TV show QI and Not the nine o'clock news. Producer of Blackadder. Co-author of the Meaning of Liff.

Hamlet: William Shakespeare - Hamlet, Act III, Scene 1, Line 56 - The soliloquy.

Superman or Kal-El: Superman is a DC Comics character created by Jerry Siegel and Joe Shuster, first appearing in "Action Comics" in 1938.

Dactyloscopy: The science of fingerprint identification.

The duodenum: The duodenum in the small intestine was named for being 12 inches or fingers long.

Sir Humphrey: The quintessential English civil servant from the "Yes Minister and Yes Prime Minister" books and TV show created by Antony Jay and Jonathan Lynn. "I explained that we are calling the white paper Open Government because you always dispose of the difficult bit in the title. It does less harm there than on the statute books." Sir Humphrey Appleby.

Chapter 20: In the pub

The Unbelievable Truth: BBC radio show hosted by David Mitchell and created by Graeme Garden and Jon Naismith.

ADHD: Attention Deficit Hyperactivity Disorder.

Chapter 22: The Work Party

Mr Bigglesworth: Hairless cat held by Dr Evil in the Austin Powers "Goldmember" movie. The cat playing Mr Bigglesworth was really called Ted Nude-Gent.

Frogger: 1981 arcade game developed by Konami and made by Sega. The aim was to get a series of frogs across a busy street and river.

Chapter 23: The Knock on the Door

Quentin Crisp: Quentin Crisp was famous for his refusal to do any housework. Author of "The Naked Civil Servant".

Chapter 25: Edward Andrews

An infinite regression: A series of appropriately related elements with a first member but no last member, where each element leads to or generates the next in some sense.

Chapter 27: The Hitman

Jacques Clouseau: Accident prone protagonist of the Pink Panther series of films.

Bagheera: Rudyard Kipling's Jungle Book stories - Bagheera is the panther character who plays a significant role as Mowgli's wise mentor and protector.

Chapter 28: Reflecting

Alice Cooper: Alice Cooper (born Vincent Damon Furnier, February 4, 1948) is an American rock singer whose career spans over five decades. Famous for wearing mascara that has run.

Wim Hof: The Iceman. An extreme athlete noted for his ability to withstand low temperatures. He developed the techniques to overcome his grief in dealing with his wife's suicide after he was left alone with four kids to look after, no money and needing to be strong for his children. "The children made me survive but it was the cold that brought me back to life. It healed me".

Chapter 29: They Bought It!

This time next year we'll be millionaires: Reference to the BBC show, Only Fools and Horses starring David Jason and Nicholas Lyndhurst. Created by John Sullivan.

Chapter 30: Travelling, not knowing

The Silva Method: The Silva Method developed by Jose Silva.

Foundation: Issac Asimov's classic sci-fi series Foundation contains 7 books and recently turned into a TV series. The series deals with galactic scale issues.

Hari Seldon: The main character in the first book of the Foundation series.

The worldview of Hari Seldon: Through the science of psychohistory, he could see that the galactic empire would collapse and another empire would arise. He convinced many that by saving science and knowledge the time in the darkness between the two great civilisations could be reduced from 30,000 years to 1,000 years.

Chapter 31: Seth Barlow

Sociopath: Personality disorder manifesting in extreme antisocial attitudes and behaviour.

Psychopath: Chronic mental disorder with abnormal or violent social behaviour. The terms are no longer used in psychology. They are now combined under the umbrella term "anti-social behaviour".

Chapter 32: The editor calls

Hit and run accidents: In the US it is estimated that about 80,000 people are hit by a vehicle each year. (That certainly seems a lot for one vehicle and is an extremely unfortunately worded statistic)

Chapter 33: The 24th floor of the Andrews Building

Fractional Reserve Banking: A banking system in which financial institutions are required to hold only a fraction of customer deposits in reserve as cash or as deposits with the central bank. The rest of the deposited funds can be used by the bank to make loans and investments.

Chapter 35: Officer Churchward problems

Wind in the Willows: Beloved children's book published in 1908 by Kenneth Grahame about the adventures of the characters Mole, Ratty, Toad and Badger.

Chapter 37: Surveillance from Barlow

The watchers are watching the watcher: Attributed to the roman poet and satirist Juvenal (c. 55 – 127 AD) - "*Quis custodiet ipsos custodes?*" usually translated as "*Who watches the watchers?*"

Chapter 40: A Clue

Gerald: Gerald the Gorilla reference. "When I caught him he was completely wild. Wild! I was livid!" Not the nine o'clock news.

Chapter 44: Fire

Arthur Dent: Protagonist in Hitchhiker's guide to the galaxy.

Hugh Hefner: Founder of Playboy magazine

Shaun of the Dead: 2004 zombie comedy film by Edgar Wright, starring Simon Pegg and Nick Frost.

Acknowledgements

Thanks to the many people who have helped me create this book series. Some helped by reading and commenting on versions of the manuscripts and some through general help and encouragement. Michele and Bill, Scott and Kat, Teresa and Tony, Pete and Helga, Pete, Karen, Dad and Sharyn, Mike and Anna, Eb. Thank you for your support, thoughts and feedback. Apologies if I missed anyone, I'll include you in the next version.

Finally to Ray and Bernie, whose kindness and generosity when I needed it the most, allowed me to complete the final publishing steps.

Thank you all.

For more information and merch including
Ray's T-Shirt Collection,

please visit

smilingtigermedia.com

www.ingramcontent.com/pod-product-compliance
Lightning Source LLC
Chambersburg PA
CBHW020343220726
48290CB00013B/535

9781763709911